DANGER ZONE

SHARON KIMBRA WALSH

Danger Zone
ISBN # 978-1-83943-907-0
©Copyright Sharon Kimbra Walsh 2020
Cover Art by Louisa Maggio ©Copyright August 2020
Interior text design by Claire Siemaszkiewicz
Totally Bound Publishing

DANGER ZONE

Dedication

To my dad and my husband,
My own real-life heroes

A mighty pain to love it is,
And 'tis a pain that pain to miss;
But of all pains, the greatest pain
It is to love, but love in vain.

Abraham Cowley
The Poems of Abraham Cowley

Chapter One

The beginning

Lieutenant junior grade Sarah Morgan stopped where the concrete quay met pitted bitumen and gazed around her. Her stomach churned with excitement and apprehension, and she thought she might be sick. She took in a deep breath of salty air, let it out and willed the nausea to abate before she made a fool of herself.

In front of her, pier nine extended approximately seven hundred and fifty feet into the sun-spangled cobalt water. Barnacles encrusted wooden pilings that supported its length and seaweed — brought in by the ebb and flow of tides — entwined and floated in undulating mounds beneath it.

Faded in places from constant exposure to the unforgiving sunlight, the asphalt was scarred by tire marks, and small puddles of oil shimmered in a myriad of rainbow colors in the sun's rays.

Thick, ridged cables, pipes and mooring ropes lay coiled untidily, as if cast aside and forgotten, while, at the end, bright yellow drums piled in a haphazard fashion leaned in a precarious stack over the water, looking unstable enough for a slight knock to send them tumbling to the seabed.

Sarah moved her gaze halfway along the jetty's length until she caught sight of the *USS BIA* moored at her berth.

That's my ship! This is for real.

Her heart skipped a beat and she shivered with nervous anticipation. For the next several months she would be stationed aboard the destroyer as part of her crew. Despite extensive training and her promotion to junior officer rank, her previous role in the United States Navy had consisted of desk jobs. Her deployment to the ship would be her first tour of duty at sea.

Usually impulsive, Sarah had uncharacteristically thought long and hard before she'd decided to change the course of her naval career. Once she'd made her decision, she'd completed the paperwork then waited—with an almost painful eagerness—to see whether her request would be granted.

Her transfer had been approved, but when she'd received her new orders, she'd been surprised to discover that her initial enthusiasm and excitement had waned. Any confidence she'd had that she could do the job had turned to self-doubt.

She questioned whether deployment to a warship was a logical and sensible way forward for her. She'd wanted to serve out the rest of her career to the best of her ability—even rise through the ranks, if possible— but she had no idea what would happen if she couldn't meet the high standards set by the United States Navy or she failed to achieve her own personal goals. She'd begun to second-guess herself and wondered if she'd made the right choice.

To make matters worse, she'd hoped her induction into life on a military vessel would have given her time—even if short—to settle into her new role. She should've known it wasn't going to be that easy.

Leading up to this day, she'd had a sinking feeling that she was going to be thrown in at the deep end. That was confirmed when she'd been advised that the USS BIA would only be in homeport for five days for maintenance and repairs before setting out on a week's shakedown training patrol, prior to being deployed on a fleet mission.

Furthermore, the ship's immediate future included operational combat duties or they could be called up at any time and sent on assignment to serve in a foreign country.

Sarah nibbled her bottom lip. *So why in the hell did I request a transfer from a nice, safe desk job to hazardous sea duty?*

She forced the troubled thoughts from her mind and stared at the battlefield-gray destroyer. The ship was moored stern-first in her berth, her sleek and sharp-edged bow pointing toward the horizon. Slothful swells churned beneath her hull and she dipped and swayed at her tethers with effortless grace.

Now and again, a large comber crested under her and the vessel reared her prow skyward and tugged at her restraints. Sarah thought it was like watching a wild animal struggling to break free from its incarceration so it could run and hunt or, in the *BIA*'s case, race the waves.

The ship stirred her elegant bulk to a silent melody that only it could hear and Sarah heard a faint noise of something heavy rolling across a hidden deck and banging into metal with a jarring and discordant clatter.

A loose object could cause untold damage to sensitive equipment and her sympathies were with the individual who had left it untethered. Careless and negligent acts were not tolerated in the Navy, and the person responsible would likely receive a severe dressing-down — or perhaps a harsher punishment — once it was discovered.

A soft and gentle breeze tainted with a briny smell and overlaid with an odor of rotting seaweed blew in from the sea. The scent assaulted Sarah's nose and her eyes watered. She tasted salt and a heavy, pungent tang of oil.

A herring gull screeched overhead and she tilted her head to watch it hovering above her in a cloudless blue sky. With wings swept back in a vee-shape and head lowered, the bird rode the wind currents, its keen vision surveying the pellucid surface, tracking its next meal and biding its time before it struck.

Close by came the thud and roar from heavy machinery, the clang of a hammer as it struck metal and raised voices intermixed with the slap of waves against ships' hulls and wharf supports.

Sarah noticed two tugboats — used to maneuver vessels by pushing or towing them to their moorings — out in the Hampton Roads channel, pulling and nudging a battleship to her berth alongside another pier. Dwarfed by the huge warship, they bobbed like toys in her boiling wake as her huge screws on slow reverse engines brought her into homeport.

Sarah half-turned to look over her shoulder. On arriving at Naval Station Norfolk, every man and woman had to report to Nimitz Hall, a major stopping-off point for everyone en route to ships, aircraft squadrons and bases overseas.

Sarah had arrived with little time to spare to be processed through the Transient Personnel Unit and catch a shuttle to take her to the *BIA*. In her rush to board the coach, she'd only managed to catch a glimpse of the sprawling naval installation. Now, like a child on its first visit to an amusement park, she swiveled full circle and tried to absorb as many different sights and sounds as she could.

Battleships, destroyers and submarines were moored in their berths at jetties to either side and in the distance. She studied them and called to mind some facts she'd read about the naval base.

With a known serving population of nine thousand and with seventy-five ships at any one time berthed alongside fourteen piers, it was easily the largest naval installation in the world.

Sarah was determined not to be late on her first day. She faced the destroyer then glanced at her watch. Butterflies danced in her stomach when she saw that twenty minutes remained before she had to report for duty.

Perspiration dampened her hands and her sea bag almost slipped from her grasp. She gripped the handles tighter and strode toward the warship. When she drew nearer and was able to see the vessel more clearly, pride coursed through her veins.

A gangway spanned a narrow channel of churning water—from pier to quarterdeck—and she stopped a short distance from it. The *USS BIA*'s hull dwarfed her, even though the ship was small compared to a battleship or an aircraft carrier. To Sarah, the ship's sweeping lines and symmetry were both forbidding and beautiful.

She'd read somewhere that the ship had been christened after a Greek goddess. Her name meant 'spirit of force, power and might, bodily strength and compulsion' and the vessel's brooding presence was evidence that she lived up to the meaning behind her title.

An article Sarah had read as to why ships were universally known as females made her smile. '*A ship is called a she because there's usually a gang of men about her. She has a waist and stays, it takes a lot of paint to keep her good-looking and she needs an experienced man to handle her correctly. Without a man at the helm, she's uncontrollable. When coming into a port, she shows her topsides, hides her bottom and heads straight for the buoys.*'

Sarah was inclined to believe in a more romantic notion of a 'ship as a she' as stemming from the tradition of boat-owners — typically and historically male — naming their vessels after significant females in their lives — wives, sweethearts and mothers.

Sarah glanced at her watch once more. She had a little time left before she needed to report aboard her new home, so she gazed up at the lofty bridge with its multiple slanted windows on three sides reflecting the bright sunlight. She was stunned at its size.

The superstructure dwarfed a Light Airborne Multi-Purpose System helicopter at rest on a helipad close to the squared-off stern, its rotor blades tied down to prevent damage from the wind.

She tracked her eyes along the hull from stern to bow, where the ship's number — one-sixteen — was painted in white. Once she'd received her orders, she'd bought as many books about the destroyer as she could lay her hands on.

Specifications, weapons and armament statistics now tumbled through her head and she went over everything she'd learned about the warship.

The *BIA* was a United States Arleigh Burke-class guided-missile destroyer and formed part of a carrier strike group. Her primary mission was to protect the designated carrier she'd been assigned to and fill an anti-aircraft combat role with her stealth techniques, using her missile defense system, anti-surface warfare launchers, powerful multifunction radar and a vertical launch system. She could launch a destructive force of heavy ordnance, such as the Tomahawk, anti-submarine rockets and evolved Sea Sparrow missiles.

Beautiful she might be, Sarah thought, *but she's also one hell of a dangerous bitch.*

Sarah stared at the main deck, where a five-inch, sixty-two-caliber gun sat forward of the bridge, its long barrel pointed skyward, then moved her gaze onward to the vast tripod main mast.

With its intricate passive array antenna, search and rescue aerial and surface gunfire control radar, it towered above the ship's superstructure and resembled a mad creator's warped idea of a steel sculpture.

Sarah's heart raced and she drew in a deep breath. She checked her watch for the third time and saw that she had five minutes left before she lost her freedom. She was out of time, so while she continued to study the bridge, she proceeded toward the gangway.

She'd almost reached it when she noticed someone staring at her through one of the windows. She gasped with surprise, stopped, stepped backward in shock and her heavy bag collided with her legs. She stumbled, almost fell and swore out loud before she regained her footing then glanced around to see if someone had overheard her profanity.

She was still alone, and she turned her attention back to the vessel and raised her hand to shield her eyes from the harsh sunlight. The slanted glass panes of the bridge were tinted gold-green with anti-glare material. The phenomenon prevented her from seeing anything other than the silhouette of a tall man dressed in a multi-blue digital naval working uniform.

Sarah confirmed that even though he must have noticed she'd seen him, the unknown male still watched her, and her anxiety increased two-fold.

Oh, shit. I must have done something wrong. He's making notes so he can ream me out – and I haven't even boarded yet. This is so not good.

Perhaps she'd broken some ancient naval tradition by not boarding the ship as soon as she'd arrived. It was too late now and she was annoyed with herself for screwing up on her first day.

Furthermore, one of her pet hates – and an irritation that was almost top of her 'things guaranteed to piss Sarah off' list – was being stared at. If she was in for a roasting, she knew she would only dig herself a deeper hole if she reacted to the man's scrutiny, so she ignored him, drew her shoulders back and proceeded to the gangway.

The muscles in her legs trembled and her heart pounded. She'd never taken part in the naval custom of saluting the ensign and the officer of the deck – OOD – an act of courtesy to the flag and the *USS BIA*. She had to draw on all her courage not to turn tail and run.

At the foot of the narrow walkway, Sarah placed her bag on the ground. She reminded herself that the man on the bridge might still be watching, and as she had no idea who he was or whether he was someone of rank, she was determined not to make a mistake.

The officer of the deck eyed her as he stood at parade rest on the quarterdeck. Without thinking about what she had to do, she stood to attention and saluted him smartly.

"Permission to come aboard, sir?" she asked.

The confidence in her voice made her feel a little smug and her lips twitched with the beginnings of a self-satisfied smile. At the last minute she thought it might be inappropriate to be seen grinning like a Cheshire cat, so she clenched her jaw and gritted her teeth.

The officer straightened and returned her salute. "Come aboard," he ordered.

Sarah picked up her sea bag and stepped on to the narrow walkway, her boots ringing on the metal surface as she ascended a slight incline. Before she walked onto the deck, she performed an about-turn to face aft, where the ensign flapped in the breeze, and she saluted for a second time.

She then rotated one-hundred and eighty-degrees to confront the OOD once more and rendered a third snappy salute that would have done her proud at Navy boot camp.

"Permission to come aboard, sir?" she asked once more.

The OOD responded immediately, "Permission to come aboard granted."

Sarah sighed with relief. It appeared she'd passed the simple but meaningful naval ceremony test and she moved onto the quarterdeck, nodded at the officer and strode at a brisk pace toward the dogged open hatch that led into the *BIA*.

As she entered the darkness lurking inside, Sarah had an unbidden thought.

Into the depths of hell go I.

Chapter Two

Captain Jack Chalmers, commanding officer of the *USS BIA*, climbed the first of two narrow metal ladders that would take him to the bridge. His keen gaze scanned the bulkheads for any problems while he listened hard to see if he could detect any abnormal sounds from the engines.

The dull gray steel of the walls showed nothing to concern him and the metal stairs remained level under his boots. To confirm matters, he stopped halfway up the second set of steps and rested his palm on the wall.

The metal was cool and a faint vibration bled into his hand and traveled along his arm. If anyone had asked him for an explanation of what it meant, he would have said it was his ship's lifeforce. While he felt the constant smooth resonance beneath his touch, all was well.

Jack had served two decades aboard military vessels, but each time he went to sea and was subjected to the sounds and smells of a warship, the sensory onslaught still had the power to stir him.

His senses had been honed by his years in the Navy, and he could tell the engines were running at half-ahead and the destroyer was plowing straight and true into light seas. She was as steady as a rock, except when her prow dipped into a trough between waves or a large breaker hit her portside and she rolled to starboard.

Apart from his mother and sisters, the *BIA* had been the only other female in his life for a long time. At the thought that she was his to command—even if she was as temperamental and as highly strung as a thoroughbred racehorse—pride swept through him.

The ship demanded—as a military vessel capable of rendering a destructive force beyond imagination—the respect and admiration of himself and everyone who served aboard her. She was his pride and joy, and eagerness seized his gut as he ascended to his domain, the navigational hub of the ship.

Jack climbed the final ladder and stepped onto the bridge. As soon as he appeared, the master chief on watch announced, "Captain on the bridge."

The men and women stopped what they were doing and snapped to attention. Jack acknowledged each of his crew while he made his way around the computers, tables and other equipment toward his chair next to the executive officer's in front of the leading edge of the windows.

He saw *her* as he approached and his stomach muscles contracted, as if from an impending punch. A mix of emotions swept through him—surprise, excitement and sexual arousal. He swallowed and his heart began to race.

He'd first seen her on pier nine when he'd watched her walk toward then stop in front of the destroyer. He'd been confident that she wouldn't be able to see him through the unusual hue of the glass, but he'd been too arrogant in his assumption.

When the expression of childlike wonder on her beautiful face had changed to one of annoyance and she'd stumbled backward in surprise, he'd stepped to the side and out of sight. It'd been too late.

Jack wondered now if she would recognize him and what her reaction would be at meeting the person who had checked her out in such a blatant manner. His behavior at being caught staring at her could have landed him in big trouble but, at the time, that had been the furthest thing from his mind.

Once she'd gone from his view, he'd been uneasy as to why he'd been compelled to stare at her for so long. He now knew why he had.

Up close, she was lovely. She remained at attention, a startled expression on her face, a faint blush staining her cheeks. Her burnished brunette hair — even pulled as it was into the severe style the Navy rules required — emphasized her heart-shaped features. Her eyes were hazel in color, with the longest, darkest lashes he'd ever seen on a woman, and she had a kissable mouth enhanced by full, moist lips.

Jack was aware that his scrutiny was bordering on being rude but he couldn't drag his gaze away. Their eyes locked and he watched the woman lick her lower lip. A shudder traced its way along his spine and a pleasurable ache coiled in his groin. His pace faltered in his walk across the deck.

During his earlier years and while rising through the ranks, he'd had a few brief relationships, but he'd never had the urge to settle down. In fact, he'd been the 'love 'em and leave 'em' type and wasn't proud of it. He could handle any ship, plan and carry out combat missions skillfully and competently, but the thought of getting married and having a family scared him shitless.

His body's response to the young lieutenant was disconcerting. The strong and obsessive attraction he had for her set his teeth on edge. He was too old to have such potent sexual longings for a woman under his command, and she was far too young to be the recipient. Of more importance to him was the fact that he would be breaking every known naval regulation concerning fraternization.

Jack dismissed the feelings she evoked in him as being nothing more than a brief and fanciful lust that a hot-blooded man might have for a gorgeous female.

He tried to keep his mind focused on the job at hand, and as he reached his chair but before he took his seat, he turned to her and said, "At ease, Lieutenant, and welcome aboard."

The woman smiled at him and any further words he wanted to say locked in his throat as she said in a voice that slid through his body like silken honey, "Thank you, sir."

Holy shit.

Jack suddenly found himself as horny as a teenager. A faint flowery scent, which he was sure was from her perfume, assailed his nostrils and tantalized his senses. His penis stirred and stiffened.

From out of the corner of his eye, he watched the lieutenant face the bow and pick up binoculars. She brought the lenses to her eyes and gazed through them, and he studied her profile, forgetting for a moment where he was.

Get a grip, dickhead. This is not the time or the place, and even if it was, it wouldn't be with her.

Struggling to rein in his rebellious thoughts and bring his libido under control, Jack said, "Helmsman. I have the conn and the bridge."

While he waited for a response to confirm his order, he remained aware of the woman's presence beside him. He had no idea what the hell was going on with him, but he had a sinking feeling he was going to find out soon enough.

Chapter Three

Six months later

Jack surveyed the vast and dimly lit ballroom, his keen gaze coming to rest on several women with long, brown hair.

He knew who he was searching for and a small dissenting voice in the back of his mind protested at what he was doing. He was asking for trouble. If by chance someone noticed his gaze lingering overly long on a female, he was in no doubt that shipboard scuttlebutt would seize the juicy piece of gossip, add tails and legs and the facts would become grossly exaggerated.

As a result, he was sure there would be raised eyebrows and questions asked as to why the stoic and impassive commander had suddenly turned into a letch.

Jack didn't give a damn. He'd struggled for months with his turbulent emotions in relation to one woman—

his new lieutenant—and to date, they'd shown no sign of retreating.

Since he'd first laid eyes on her, her face had remained etched in his mind. The feelings she'd stirred in him surprised him with their strength and depth and an unfamiliar turmoil had taken up residence in his head.

They were a constant and pathetic reminder that he was forty-two years old and as naïve as a newborn regarding the opposite sex.

To make matters worse, as time had passed and she'd continued to haunt not only his waking hours but also his dreams, his body had taken a perverse delight in betraying him at the most inopportune moments during her watches on the bridge.

His thoughts were annoyingly detailed and he'd forgotten what it was like to feel *normal*. He'd tried to distance himself with work—however, the images spawned by his brief glimpses of her and the short but frequent contact between them tormented him, no matter what he did.

Jack had attempted to avoid her, but the close confines of the ship made that impossible. Furthermore, everyone onboard, including himself, was under scrutiny by one or more people twenty-four hours a day, which made the situation even more embarrassing.

In his eyes, it was both unprofessional and perverse of him to think about a young woman in his charge in the way he did, let alone someone eighteen years his junior. The situation bordered on the ridiculous.

Jack had always followed the Navy rule book to the letter. He was a man dedicated to protocol and the chain of command. He believed wholeheartedly in everything the military stood for. Based on those ethics, he enforced regulations to the last word and expected his crew to follow his example.

Of late, things had changed. Sarah Morgan had crashed into his life with the force of an explosion. He wanted to spend more time with her and get to know her better, and it didn't matter how he tried to suppress his longing for her or convince himself that his feelings were futile. It was wrong to want her, but his self-control was waning and common sense had flown out of the window.

He was fighting a losing battle. His heart continued to force him on a course he thought would eventually lead him to do something he might later regret. His helplessness at his loss of control had left him needing one hell of a big shovel to dig himself free of the pile of virtual shit he'd become buried in.

Jack attempted to dismiss Lieutenant Sarah Morgan from his mind and focus on more important issues. The USS BIA's last sea duty had consisted of fleet patrols in the Mediterranean Sea. They'd been particularly arduous. They'd lasted six months, and by the time he'd brought her into homeport, she was long overdue for maintenance and simple repairs to be done on some of her equipment, which had begun to malfunction on the journey home.

More importantly, his crew had needed shore leave before their next operation. Once he'd berthed the destroyer, he'd worked out a simple system whereby rotating teams each spent forty-eight hours on the ship, so they could all have some downtime.

That day, he'd ordered a disgruntled skeleton staff to stay onboard and allowed the remaining men and women a short furlough so they could take part in Naval Station Norfolk's centenary celebrations.

In relation to his own tasks, the lack of command responsibilities had given Jack an opportunity to complete paperwork and oversee engineers. He'd also been able to attend the ball arranged for his men and women as part of the numerous parties they'd not been able to participate in while out at sea without neglecting his duties.

In his mind's eye, Jack saw the clean-cut lines of his ship. He pictured how her bow cleaved its way through heavy seas and the way her helm responded to quick changes in course. She was *his* and he'd always placed his duty to protect her and all those who served aboard her high on his list of priorities.

That was until another female had entered his life.

Jack ceased to contemplate his past and his brooding on the present and studied his surroundings. The party going on around him was in full swing, with his crew taking advantage of their freedom, which had been severely curtailed during their time at sea.

He grinned when he noticed that everyone seemed intent on expending their excessive energy by creating as much noise as possible and drinking the bar dry.

He had no intention of ruining their night, but he hoped that sinking a few beers — and more-than-likely spirits — wouldn't leave some hammered and unable to perform their duties on the ship the next day when they reported in for a crew changeover.

Such an occurrence might lead him to discipline a few for being late back or hungover. He'd never been keen on punishment. It disrupted morale and the combat readiness of the ship, and created an uncomfortable atmosphere among ratings and officers. It was something he intended to avoid at all costs.

Even more importantly, he wanted to prevent such an incident occurring before they weighed anchor. At fourteen hundred hours in five days' time, the *BIA* would leave homeport for a week's shakedown shore patrol to test refurbished equipment and check final repairs.

Jack could only hope everyone would report aboard sober, with their Navy heads on straight, and be ready to resume their duties.

There she is.

Chapter Four

Like a ship's missile locking on to a heat signature, Jack's gaze fastened on Sarah Morgan.

Three women were already on the floor, and when she started to dance alongside them, his body tensed. A dull ache coalesced in his groin and the muscles there tightened to form a pleasurable knot.

He'd always thought he was a typical hot-blooded male with normal sexual feelings and responses to a beautiful woman. He'd never experienced such an intense physical attraction as he had to her, though. After seeing her tonight, a fire burned in his gut and there was only one way to put it out.

Jack took in her glossy curls that spread in a mouth-watering cascade over her shoulders. He watched her laugh and toss wayward tendrils from her face, and a compulsive need to have her ran through him.

Her slim figure was clothed in a pale green strapless dress, the skirt floating like gossamer about her legs. Crystal beads embellished the pleated top and clung to and outlined her full breasts. The style emphasized her slim waist and he caught a glimpse of a long, tan leg through a hip-high slit in her skirt. The fire in his groin ramped up to a white-hot blaze.

He knew her name but, like a stalker, he'd gleaned further information about her from her personnel file.

She was twenty-four, five feet ten inches tall and weighed around one hundred forty pounds. She had six years' outstanding service in the Navy and was accredited with a long list of achievements and qualifications. She exhibited excellent leadership skills and qualities, and he believed she could pass any promotion examinations she set her mind to.

Jack knew other things as well. When she spoke to him, even though it was only in relation to her role on the destroyer, his stomach quaked with nervous excitement like he was a gauche schoolboy experiencing his first crush.

On the odd occasion that he was forced to pass by her in the narrow passageways, he'd been gripped with an irresistible urge to grab her and kiss her senseless.

After seeing and meeting her, he'd known he would have to keep his distance. Whenever she was near, she made him feel like he'd been starving for someone like her his whole life. Her mere existence had given him a taste of something he hadn't known he'd needed.

"She's some looker, isn't she?"

A voice spoke in Jack's ear. It distracted him and irritation surged through him at the interruption. He turned to find Commander Chad Mason, his executive officer, beside him and he asked curtly, "What? Who?"

"Need you ask?" Chad replied and gestured with his head at the dance floor. "*The* Lieutenant Morgan."

Jack wasn't sure whether his XO had noticed that he was paying far too much attention to the woman in question, and he was uneasy at the thought.

Jack glared at his friend. "I've not really noticed her," he said and sipped his ice-filled water.

"Yeah, okay, if you say so. But you *are* drooling, buddy. Can't say I blame you though. Ship scuttlebutt says she has her own fan club."

Jack tightened his lips in a grimace. "Screw you, Mason."

His gaze returned to the instigator of his turmoil and he continued to stare at her.

She is *gorgeous.*

His heart beat fast and unevenly and longing wrenched his vitals. The sensation was replaced with a sharp stab in his gut as a man walked to the lieutenant's side, bent his head and spoke to her.

Jack gritted his teeth and his body tensed. He watched Sarah Morgan flick hair from her face with her hand and respond to the conversation with far too much attentiveness. He hated what it might mean for him.

The male was not only young and good-looking but an officer in command of one of four reaction force teams on the *BIA*. Jack wondered if he was going to capture her attention for himself.

The muscles in his stomach twisted themselves into a tangle at the thought and a bitter emotion swept through him. For a moment, he couldn't put a name to it, until the man touched the woman's arm and the feeling intensified into an adolescent resentment.

I'm jealous.

A memory transported his mind back in time to when he had been fourteen years old. Another kid —

one he'd had the misfortune to be involved with in constant yard fist fights ever since he'd started high school—had monopolized a girl whom Jack secretly had the hots for.

The boy had repeatedly taunted him on the subject and one day Jack lost his temper and had punched him in the face. The anger he now felt was similar and urged him to deal with the young officer in the same way. It made him feel as out of control as it had then.

He was tired of fighting the emotions Sarah Morgan had innocently generated in him. He knew he had to rein in his rebellious feelings, relax and start to mingle with his crew and officers. He needed to enjoy the short break away from naval obligations while he could.

His mind and body had other ideas, however, and he remained fixated on the woman. He couldn't help but notice the way her hips swayed to the music in a sexy manner and the erotic glimpse of her femininely muscled leg through the gap in her dress.

His lips twisted in a grimace when he realized he was at a complete loss as to how to get out of the swamp of desire he was beginning to drown in.

Chapter Five

Sarah swept tendrils of hair away from her face and smiled at the man with her. He was obviously trying to impress her by performing some fast and intricate dance steps.

The music was loud, so she leaned toward him so he could hear her. "I'm impressed, Mike. Are there any more moves where those came from?"

Lieutenant Mike Stevens touched her arm. "Lots more, honey. Wanna come outside with me so I can show you?"

A mock leer contorted his tan features and Sarah's smile widened. "Like hell I will. I'd like to keep my virtue safe. Thanks for the offer though."

Mike shrugged at her words, grabbed her hand in his and spun her around. Sarah tossed her head back and laughed out loud.

She was aware that the young officer had a crush on her, because he'd never made any attempt to hide the fact. Each time they met — and sometimes she thought he'd planned those encounters—his chocolate-colored eyes roamed her face and body and he flirted with her outrageously.

He'd never been shy about using his charms on her at every opportunity either. Without fail, his attractive white-toothed smile had tried to coax a response from her each time he'd stopped to speak to her.

Sarah thought he was a nice-enough guy. He was good-looking to boot, but she'd met his type before and reached the conclusion that he was too full of himself. She was sure that women—no matter their age—fell at his feet in droves and she didn't intend to become another notch on his bed post.

Since being stationed on the *USS BIA*, she'd been asked out on so many dates that she'd lost count. She'd turned down each one and provided herself with numerous reasons for her cool reaction with each man.

She'd started to wonder about her negative reactions to Mike and other men. In recent weeks she'd finally admitted to herself that she had no interest in a relationship, except the one she wanted.

He was so far out of her reach that he might as well have been on another planet. Her confusion as to how she could handle her feelings had made her reluctant to embark on an affair with anyone else.

Sarah responded with a lighthearted teasing as most normal women might to flirtatious advances made by a handsome naval lieutenant and she continued to dance on.

She had to force herself to do so because her heart wasn't in it. All she could think about was a man with salt-and-pepper hair, impassive features and an unapproachable persona. He remained uppermost in her mind and her thoughts refused to leave her in peace.

When she was on duty, each time she was close to him or she had cause to pass him in other areas of the ship, his presence invariably induced a shy verbal response when he spoke to her—and more disturbingly, an undeniable erotic warmth to spread throughout her body.

She wasn't inexperienced in relation to men by any means, but on more than one occasion when they had both been on the bridge, her face had burned with a blush at the images evoked by him. She'd found herself struggling to breathe, as if all the oxygen had been sucked from the atmosphere.

If the feelings were nothing more than an intense sexual attraction, they were like none she'd experienced before. Furthermore, a voice of reason screamed in her mind that there was no way she could be attracted to or have fallen for a man who was a stranger to her.

It didn't happen that way for her. She needed to get to know somebody first, then love came later—or so Sarah tried to convince her traitorous mind and body, with little success.

She tried to forget about the man who haunted her every waking moment and concentrate on her partner. She was determined to enjoy herself if it was the last thing she did, because it had been months since she'd had the opportunity to don a dress and wear high-heeled shoes.

While she felt like a woman once more out of her working uniform, the freedom and relaxation she got when she listened to music or danced while out socially were nowhere to be found. Her thoughts were sluggish, her body listless and emptiness lay like a lead ball in her stomach, confirmation that someone or something was missing from her life.

Dammit. If only he was with me…

Sarah's uneasy thoughts disappeared when Mike grabbed her hands once more and whirled her around. Enjoyment finally swept over her, which lasted until she glanced over his shoulder and saw *him*.

Oh. Shit.

The sight of him made her lose her composure as well as her rhythm and she missed her footing. She regained her balance and stepped to her left so she could see the man who had made her both mentally and physically giddy.

Jack Chalmers, aka the captain and commanding officer of the *USS BIA*, or 'the ole man' or 'ole frosty', as some of the crew had nicknamed him.

Sarah had heard about him even before she'd joined the ship. He had a reputation for being one of the best senior-ranking officers in the Navy. He'd served in Iraq and Afghanistan and he'd been decorated many times.

Shipboard gossip said he wasn't remotely interested in women and had a love affair going on with his ship. In addition, he was a badass officer when it came to sea warfare and tactical and strategic planning. Furthermore, she'd heard that he possessed integrity and values beyond reproach. Those traits alone put him out of her league.

It doesn't matter. I want him like hell or I'm acting like a bitch in heat for a man I want but can't have.

Sarah's heart flipped and her insides turned somersaults when the man under her scrutiny nodded in her direction. Flustered, she stumbled again but regained her balance and studied him in his white service summer uniform.

In the past, she'd noticed how tall he was and now she guessed his height to be well over six feet. His tunic fit his broad chest and shoulders perfectly, the tailoring emphasizing his slim waist. Knife-edged creased pants outlined his muscular thighs and tapered elegantly to white dress shoes.

Black shoulder boards with gold braid showed his rank. A naval pin and rows of ribbons above his left breast pocket were the only colors marring his pristine uniform.

Sarah's throat went dry and she swallowed. She forgot she was supposed to be dancing with Mike and was surrounded by her shipmates. Any one of them couldn't fail to notice how her gaze was wholly fixed on the man who stood a short distance from her. She didn't want to become the subject of shipboard rumor, but at that moment she didn't care.

I'm heading for trouble if I carry on like this. But I want him so much.

Jack Chalmers half-turned to speak to a man beside him, whom she recognized as Commander Chad Mason. She lost eye contact with him, and when the two men walked away, disappointment stabbed her.

She froze when, before he disappeared into the crowd, he glanced over his shoulder at her. Their gazes locked and a frisson of emotion crackled between them. Sarah shivered.

He vanished among the people congregated at the bar and she was left breathless and wondering whether what had happened had been a figment of her imagination.

She wouldn't be the first or the last woman to fall for a man who was unobtainable. Still, she berated herself for the faint hope she felt because of the way he'd looked at her. After all, she was a lowly lieutenant junior grade who had the hots for her commanding officer, and she knew he wouldn't jeopardize his career by showing any interest in her.

Sarah noticed that the music had stopped. She glanced around and discovered Mike had left her alone. Her cheeks flushed with embarrassment, and when one of the three women she'd come to the ball with caught her attention, she rejoined her.

She sank onto a chair, sighing with relief at being able to rest her aching feet. She'd only been seated for a few moments when another song began to play and two of her companions rushed back onto the floor.

"Wanna dance?" her long-time friend, Babs Forrester, asked.

"I think I'll sit this one out," Sarah replied and lifted her feet to wave them to and fro. "These feel like they've got concrete blocks attached to them. Go on. I'll be here when you get back."

Babs returned to the floor and Sarah watched her friend's hips twitch and sway with exaggerated sexiness in response to the sixties track now playing. She sighed and wished she could throw herself into the spirit of things and enjoy the party.

In need of a drink, she eyed the littered tabletop and managed to find her glass of iced water among the other half-drank and empty ones crowded together on its surface. Once she'd found it, she sipped the cold liquid, a shiver slipping through her when chilled moisture doused her throat and eased the dryness there.

She set it down and ran her finger absentmindedly through the condensation on its sides. The muscles in her neck and shoulders were tense and she couldn't relax, so she stared at the ballroom's décor and elegant furnishings.

Ultramarine light pervaded the room, rippling and shimmering like a sun-spangled sea. The color was obviously being used in honor of the Navy being present in the building and kicking up hell.

The blue-and-gold crest of the *USS BIA* was displayed on a huge screen that filled the length of one wall with its Latin inscription—*Potentia Perdere*—Power to Destroy—highlighted beneath it.

Tables draped in pristine white linen held tall, slim cerulean vases in their centers with fragrant chalky blooms cascading from them. Diaphanous sheers festooned floor-to-ceiling windows and the wall-to-wall carpet was a plush pile patterned in sapphire and lapis lazuli swirls and spirals, once again depicting water.

It was a spectacular room and Sarah knew accommodations at the Hilton Virginia Beach Oceanfront hotel were nothing to be sneezed at either. The Navy, when in town and hosting an event, spared no expense for their personnel.

Sarah felt restless and sipped her tasteless drink. A brief lull in the music reduced the noise level and her friends arrived back at their table.

Babs stopped in front of her. "We're off to the bar," she said. "It could take all night to get served, so we might need you to come and rescue us if we don't get back in an hour or so. Do you want anything?"

Sarah pointed at her glass. "Another one of these, thanks."

Babs pushed strands of blonde hair out of her face. "Okay, one iced water coming up. Behave while I'm gone, hon."

Sarah laughed and watched the woman she had known for years join the others and make their way through the throng of people at the bar.

She smiled to herself and murmured, "Good luck with that."

She searched the room but she couldn't see *him*. She presumed he'd left, and when she thought she might not see him until they set sail in a few days' time, her stomach muscles knotted painfully.

Goddammit. This is ridiculous.

The lights dimmed and slow music started to play, encouraging couples to take to the dance floor.

Sarah frowned. *Oh, well. I guess I can make like a wallflower. Or I could go outside and get some fresh air.*

A brief respite from the noise might ease the tension in her muscles and she lifted her glass to take a last drink of water.

She froze in the act, the cold rim touching her lips, a small amount of liquid spilling out to trickle down her cleavage.

Oh. Hell.

Chapter Six

Sarah's eyes opened wide in surprise because Jack Chalmers stood in front of her.

How long has he been there?

The thought vanished as quickly as it had come when he asked, "Would you like to dance, Lieutenant?"

I must be dreaming. Has someone slipped something in my drink? Have I got wrecked without my knowledge?

Her cheeks burned hot with a blush. She swallowed the mouthful of water, nodded and, with care, placed her glass on the table. She rose to her feet, and although the muscles in her legs trembled, she managed to walk past him with her back straight and without tottering on her high heels.

He fell in behind her and she felt his hand on the small of her back. His touch sent tiny electric shocks racing up her spine and her wits scattered. It was all she could do to concentrate on putting one foot in front of the other and not face-plant on the carpet.

Once on the dance floor, she faced him and he moved close to her. He slid his arm around her waist and took her right hand in his—his touch firm and warm, palm rough—and brought it to his chest where he held it.

Tingles stung her fingertips, built in strength and raced to her shoulder. A wild tremor went through her and every nerve in her body thrummed.

They swayed to the love song and Sarah felt him exhale on the highly sensitive skin of her forehead. His thighs pressed against hers and the spicy odor of his cologne assailed her nostrils. She felt lightheaded, as though she'd drunk too much liquor, and her senses went into overdrive.

To be so close to him was a thing she'd thought would never happen. The sexual attraction she had for him sent heat coursing through her. Her nerves ignited, leaving her aroused and needing more. Any restraint she might have had in relation to resisting his touch vanished.

The heat in her cheeks intensified and she couldn't look him in the face for fear he would see in her expression the feelings she desperately wanted to keep hidden from him. She chose instead to stare over his left shoulder.

"I don't bite, you know."

Sarah heard his murmured words and his breath caressed the delicate skin of her ear. She turned her head to look at him and noticed he was staring at her with an intense and unwavering gaze.

His mouth was only a few inches from her own and a small lump settled in her throat. She coughed. "Don't you, sir?" she asked, the last word trailing off in an unflattering squeak.

Her gaze went to his lips and a smile lifted a corner of his mouth.

"Hell, no," he replied. "Are you enjoying yourself?"

I am now, I think.

Sarah raised her eyes back to his and noticed how blue they were. For a moment she was lost in them, then she remembered his question and forced away the intimate thoughts.

Her voice was low and husky when she replied, "It's a lovely venue, sir. I've had a great time."

It would be even lovelier if you kissed me.

Her cheeks grew warmer and excitement swirled in her stomach.

Jack squeezed her hand. "Hey, I don't frighten you, do I?"

Sarah hesitated before answering. She studied his tan, clean-shaven face and square jawline and noticed he had a slight dimple in the center of his chin.

I could stare at him forever.

At last she shook her head. "No, sir, you don't. But you are my commanding officer. Aren't I supposed to be a bit afraid of you?"

His expression changed and the planes of his face hardened at her words. A muscle twitched in his jaw and she wondered whether she'd said something wrong.

For a moment he stayed silent, his eyes distant, then he grinned. "I guess I forgot who I was for a minute. Don't you know that even commanding officers can be human, Lieutenant?"

Sarah smiled in return. "I believe you, sir. But on the bridge, they can seem a bit...unapproachable."

His smile is making me imagine things I shouldn't be thinking.

"Yeah, but we're not. You should try me sometime."
Is he flirting with me or teasing me?

As if in answer to her unspoken question, he tightened his arm around her and held her closer. The increased pressure of his body against hers stirred a miniature tornado of desire inside her.

Oh. My. Lord. I need –

Jack rested his cheek on her hair and the thought flew from her mind. Her heart lurched. If she turned and moved her head, her lips would touch his skin, and if she found the courage to kiss him, she could taste him.

Their bodies swayed together in perfect harmony and she wanted to stay in his embrace for as long as she could. She yearned to tell him how she felt, but she had no idea what precisely those feelings were and she wouldn't have known where to begin. At that point, it would take more courage than she possessed.

She and Jack were bound by rules, regulations and the Navy rumor mill. If she became entangled in a relationship with him, she would be the loser.

She was stubborn, however, and when she wanted something strongly enough, she wouldn't stop until she'd succeeded in getting it. Even though the odds against her ever being able to have Jack Chalmers were overwhelmingly high, this was one of those times. She wanted him.

In a surge of recklessness, she decided to throw caution to the winds and pushed her body tentatively into his.

I'm nothing but a hooker begging for sex, but if he doesn't understand the signals I'm sending him, then I don't know what else I've got to do.

There was no response from him and embarrassment flooded through her. She'd obviously misunderstood his interest and had made a fool of herself.

It was as if the sexual side of her nature was compelling her to do things she'd never done before. She'd thrown herself at him and let him know what she was asking for. She cringed inside at what he might think of her.

Her mortification faded, however, when he rubbed his face on the side of her head. It might have been unintentional, however, because Sarah couldn't envisage Jack Chalmers being so obvious in public.

A woman's intuition was a sensory thing, however, and hers told her he *had* signaled his interest in her. Its implications made her feel as if she were teetering on the edge of an abyss and was about to fall in.

The music finished and Jack stepped backward. "Thank you, Lieutenant. That was nice."

His eyes held hers for a moment, then he inclined his head, about-turned and walked away. Sarah was left alone on the dance floor for the second time that evening, her mind whirling with confusion.

'Thank you, Lieutenant?'

'Nice?'

The polite words rang in her head and, with a last look at him, she went to join her friends, who'd arrived back from the bar with fresh drinks.

Sarah sat beside Babs and forced a smile when her friend said, "I thought I told you to behave yourself. That did look cozy though. What was it like getting up close and personal with the 'ole man'?"

Sarah shrugged nonchalantly. "Same as dancing with any commanding officer, I suppose, like being held by a robot."

She was lying through her teeth and couldn't keep up the pretense any longer. She stood and picked up her beaded purse, which hung on the back of her chair.

"Listen… I'm going outside. I need to take a walk to clear my head."

Babs' expression changed to one of concern. "Should you? Go out there on your own, I mean?"

"Babs, I'm a big girl. I can deal with the dark. Anyway, with all these hunky Navy guys around, I'm sure I'll be safe. I'd only need to scream and they'd come running to my rescue."

Sarah put a reassuring hand on her friend's shoulder, smiled and moved away. She skirted tables, excused herself through throngs of people and made her way to the frosted glass doors that led out of the ballroom. Once she reached them, she glanced over her shoulder one last time to see if she could see Jack.

He was nowhere to be found and she sighed, pressed her shoulder to the heavy barrier, pushed hard and, once it opened, stepped into the corridor that ran parallel to the room she'd left.

It was quiet, the clamor from inside indistinct and the temperature less humid. An air conditioning unit embedded in the ceiling blew a chilled blast onto her hot cheeks and she raised her face to cool her skin.

Sarah wanted to be on her own. She knew she could use an exit leading from one of the rooms to get to a deck at the rear of the hotel that led to the Virginia Beach boardwalk and the sea, and she proceeded along the hallway.

At each door, she paused to check inside to see if it was the room she sought until, farther along the passageway, she heard raucous sounds coming from the fourth opening.

She went toward it, glanced inside and saw that several members of the crew had made themselves at home on the plush leather sofas and chairs. Beyond them, she could see the exit.

Sarah went in and was immediately greeted by overly loud and drunken voices asking her to join them. She didn't want to appear rude, so she stopped to talk, all the while aware of the white wooden double doors leading out onto a large deck area where seating and benches with parasols were placed for patrons who wanted to smoke or enjoy the sea air.

Desperate for peace and quiet and eager to break loose, she edged in the direction of her escape route while continuing to smile and light-heartedly refuse the over-affectionate and zealous attentions from the males in the group.

At last, freed from further conversation and with a final wave, she made her bid for freedom through the doors and headed toward some steps. Before descending them, she kicked off her sandals, picked them up and fled.

Chapter Seven

Sarah descended the steps and hurried across the wide, wooden boardwalk. At its edge, she held up her skirt then hesitated and stared to her left along the stretch of dark beach. It looked shadowy and lonely, and doubt tugged at her. She shrugged, jumped down onto the powdery sand and headed in the direction of the sea.

Damn Captain Jack Chalmers to hell.

The control she'd had over her feelings for him had been blown out of the water during their dance. Being held in his arms had only served to stir her already-wayward emotions and sexual desire into a cauldron of heat and excitement that she knew could only be satiated by him.

Her wish to be away from her friends to clear her head was strong, but she stopped and scrunched her toes into the silken sand. It was still warm from the day's sun and she enjoyed the softness beneath her feet.

A small voice in her subconscious reminded her that she was by herself, with no help close by should she run into trouble. The disregard for her own safety that her swirling feelings added might prove to be a recipe for disaster and wouldn't solve her problems.

Sarah's frustration at the situation she found herself in forced her onward.

I'll be fine, she reassured herself. *I won't go too far.*

An image of Jack's face slid into her mind and she sighed. It was only going to get worse. It would be impossible for her to be in his company onboard the ship. She wouldn't be able to look at him without letting him see how much she cared for him and her body would continue to betray her when she was near him.

Get a grip. You're acting like a dumb schoolgirl with her first crush.

Deep in thought, she walked on, noise from the hotel fading the farther she moved away from it. When she shook herself from her reverie and glanced over her shoulder to gauge how far she'd come, the lights from the building had grown dim.

The only illumination was from the moon's rays, which glittered in a silver swathe on the sea and on the strip of sand she was on. She ignored the fact that night had encroached into her personal space and shadows had grown close, and with her head bowed, she strode on.

What do I feel for him? How can I be so screwed up when I don't even know the man?

The dry sand changed to damp beneath Sarah's feet. She raised her head to see where she was and saw the ocean a short distance in front of her. She tilted her head so she could look up at the night sky and saw a huge cream moon surrounded by a canvas of diamond-bright stars.

Moonbeams threw an incandescent radiance onto tiny rollers tipped with froth and outlined their caps with white phosphorescence as they broke on the shore. The faint hiss as they washed over the pebbles was soothing to her ears and some of the tension left her body.

At the water's edge, she turned left to walk parallel to the shore. She heard a seagull shriek above her and she thought it sounded tired and lost. She listened to see if another one would call to guide it in and felt sad when there was no response.

A soft, warm breeze entwined itself in her hair and tugged at her skirt. She smelled the sharp briny tang of ocean and kelp and watched waves swell and break apart the path of silver. She finally heard a sharp and piercing cry from a second bird and a weaker answer from the first, which made her spirits rise.

I guess I'll deal with whatever happens. It's taught me a lesson, though, never to set my sights too high.

Sarah found peace and solitude on the night-shadowed beach and moderated her pace to a stroll, swinging her sandals in one hand and her purse in the other.

She was oblivious to how far she'd gone until she noticed that, except for the moonlight splashing onto the sea, a coal-black curtain now surrounded her.

Trepidation stirred inside her. She glanced back the way she'd come and saw the hotel lights were now tiny gold halos of warmth. The sound of music had disappeared and the only noise marring the heavy silence was the splash of wavelets on the shore.

She hadn't meant to walk for so long, and when she saw how far she would have to travel to reach safety, fear stabbed at her.

Sarah didn't scare easily. She was perfectly capable of defending herself if the need arose, but she saw no reason to tempt fate now. She decided to return to the hotel and its well-lit haven, reasoning that once she was close to the deck area, she could find a spot on the sand to sit and enjoy her solitude.

The darkness — so tranquil earlier — began to shift and coalesce into imagined figures. When she turned to retrace her steps, she increased her pace, understanding how children felt when night terrors told them there were monsters under their beds.

She'd only gone a few feet when a man spoke from behind her. "Hey, sweet thang. Where ya going?"

Sarah had had a fear of spiders since she was a young child. She'd awakened one night to discover a large arachnid on her pillow, a few inches from her face. She'd jerked away from it and the creature had run straight at her. She'd become hysterical and had screamed for so long that she'd been physically sick.

On another occasion as a teenager, she'd disobeyed her parents by sneaking downstairs to watch a horror movie. It had frightened her so much she'd had nightmares for a week afterward.

But she'd *never* been as afraid as she was now. Her heart stopped for a single beat before it raced on and her breath locked in her throat.

She hadn't heard the man's approach. She could only assume she must have been so deep in thought that she'd not paid attention to her sixth sense, which had — on at least two occasions in the past — alerted her to the presence of danger.

"Hey, honey. You hear me?" The stranger spoke once more, only this time he'd drawn nearer—far too close for Sarah's comfort.

The voice was hoarse, as though the owner had smoked heavily for many years. His words were slow and slurred and it was obvious liquor had played a part in his present actions, possibly the alcohol bolstering his courage enough that he'd had the temerity to waylay her.

Her fight or flight mode suddenly overwhelmed her. Unfortunately, instead of running, she decided to fight.

She half-turned. At the same time, the moon chose to hide behind a cloud. With no time for her eyes to adapt to the sudden blackness that enveloped her, she could only see a vague outline of the man who'd spoken to her.

Sarah swallowed. "Can I help you with something?" she asked and tried to keep her voice steady.

As soon as she'd spoken, she realized she must be the dumbest woman on the planet. She tightened her grip on the straps of her shoes until they dug into her palm and she teetered on the balls of her feet, ready to run if the stranger made any hostile move toward her.

"Now that you mention it, yeah. Stop and talk with me for a bit. I'm kinda lonesome," the man answered.

Sarah shivered when she detected a faint menace underlying his words.

Shit. Stop and talk? Yeah, why not? Let's sit and shoot the shit. You've got to be fucking kidding me, buddy.

Adrenaline surged through Sarah's veins, charging her with energy to flee. She stepped backward and raised her bag in a defensive gesture, as if the flimsy pouch could prevent the stranger from coming near her.

"I have to go," she said and half-turned to run.

The moon reappeared, its silvery light bathing the beach once more. Out of the corner of her eye, she saw the man advance the few feet between them as sinuously as a snake about to attack.

Before Sarah could move, he clamped his hand onto her arm and dug sharp fingernails into her skin. Shocked at how fast the situation had deteriorated, she winced and dropped her sandals.

"Aww, stay here with me, honey. You're such a pretty thing, and all alone out here too. It must be my lucky night."

Sarah tried to pull free from the man's grip but his bony fingers tightened on her forearm. She felt the fragile bones grind together and she was dragged roughly toward him, close enough that she was able to see his face.

Wild, tangled hair straggled and covered his emaciated features and he sported a long, unkempt beard. The whites of his eyes glowed in the semi-darkness and he smiled, revealing uneven and discolored teeth. A rank odor of urine, feces and dirt drifted from his body and the miasma swirled like an invisible cloud in the air.

Sarah gagged at the smell. *Who is he? A vagrant? A rapist? A...serial killer? What does he want? I know what he wants.*

Whoever he was, he more than likely lived in the sand dunes and therefore had easy and unlimited access to the beach at night. The vast shore was his restaurant and his bar and, more sinister, the sands were his territory. He could search for unsuspecting persons hidden by the darkness whenever he wanted.

Sarah didn't care who or what he was, where he lived or why he was there, although the latter could well pertain to her and the position she was in right then.

"Let. Me. *Go!*"

Her voice was filled with desperation. The pitiful tone caused her fear to increase because, for the first time in her life, she was vulnerable and in deep trouble. She had to find the tenacity and courage to get out of the situation on her own without making matters worse and endangering her life.

She tried to pull free once more. Horror filled her when the man yanked her to his body. She dropped her bag and managed to insinuate her hand between them and push on his chest to keep him away from her.

Her palm encountered a damp and slimed outer-garment encrusted with an unimaginable mixture of noxious fluids. Sarah retched with disgust. She dreaded to think what horrific grime coated the material but the thought fled when he released her and put his arm around her waist to tug her forward.

Sarah clenched her teeth in panic. She gasped and pummeled the stranger's arm, her knuckles flaring with pain at the contact with sinewy muscle covering spindly bone.

The man growled like an animal. "Oh, you're a feisty one, all right. I like the spirited ones, I do."

Fright almost overwhelmed her. Sarah stepped to the side to put some distance between them, but despite the man's skinny build, he possessed a strength enhanced by the determination of a predator who had captured its prey and had no intention of letting it go.

"C'mon, sweetheart. Play fair. You make it easy for me and we'll get along fine. Make it hard and you might get hurt—and it'll be your fault," he said.

Sarah heard the implied threat in his words and an icy trickle ran the length of her spine. Without thinking, she brought her knee up and made direct contact with her assailant's testicles.

He squealed like a pig, but instead of crumpling to the ground as she'd hoped, she found she'd only succeeded in making him angry.

"You want it rough, bitch? Okay, we'll do rough."

Her attacker grabbed a skein of her hair and wound it around his palm. He yanked on it viciously and an intense pain pierced her scalp. Sarah bit back a scream.

She didn't dare let the noise escape in case it inflamed the man even further. To ease the agony, she leaned into him to slacken the tension.

He violently jerked the strands once more then pushed his closed fist on the top of her head and forced her to her knees.

Moisture dampened the skirt of Sarah's dress and a glacial fear consumed her. She sensed that something unspeakable was going to happen to her and she would be lucky to get out of the terrifying mess alive.

She reached a trembling hand up and grasped the man's fingers. She tried to pry them loose to ease the torment, but with sadistic brutality, he wrenched her head again. This time the agony was so intense that she let out a scream of hurt and terror.

Chapter Eight

Jack watched Sarah rise from her chair, speak briefly to one of her friends then make her way toward the exit.

Where's she going? Should I follow her or leave her alone?

He'd noticed she was shy when she hadn't been able to look at him during their dance, and he'd thought it adorable. He'd felt the tension in her body as he held her, had seen her blush and the hesitancy of her smile.

He'd been taken aback at her unexpected response, which was why he'd left her so abruptly on the dance floor. He'd felt guilty as hell for doing so.

Fate or destiny had come into play since she'd been in his arms. On reflection, there was no chance he was going to let her slip away from him now. He needed to find out what her feelings for him were, because if he knew, he could figure out what to do about his own, if anything.

His decision made, Jack placed his glass on a nearby table, put on his cap and hurried to the exit. Once he reached the doors, he pushed them open, left the ballroom and went out into the hallway.

He saw her a short distance away, peering into a room as if she were searching for someone or something. He watched and waited as she walked a few more paces before she entered a door at the end of the corridor. The moment she disappeared from his view, he followed her.

He drew close to the room she'd gone into, heard voices and knew she'd entered the Deck Room. From there, she could exit onto the boardwalk, which would take her to the beach.

Jack slowed his pace and entered the bar area, his appearance generating loud greetings and comments from his crew, who were obviously feeling the effects of too much liquor.

Some saluted him half-heartedly, others slurred incomprehensible words which, had they been on the *BIA*, would have resulted in him handing out severe reprimands for being under the influence. As it was, he was more interested in watching Sarah kick off her sandals and run down the steps into the darkness.

As far as he was aware, the hotel surroundings were supposed to be safe. There were plenty of people about, but he was still concerned for her safety, so once he'd acknowledged the inebriated calls from the crowd, he went out onto the deck.

He saw Sarah making her way toward the sea and he jogged to the topmost stair to follow her. His foot was outstretched to take the first step when he hesitated.

What the fuck am I doing?

Jack had never broken a single rule in his long career. His decision to go after her was in complete opposition to everything he'd conformed to in his forty-two years. He knew what he was about to do was wrong and his conscience screamed at him.

His job as captain and commanding officer required that he maintain his composure, keep his emotions in check, control his anger and avoid aggressive behavior, even in difficult situations. It also required honesty and ethics and that he be reliable and responsible.

If he were honest with himself, he was about to breach all those character traits, and he was torn between his duty and a desperate need for the heady and sexual excitement she could give him if she reciprocated his feelings.

He knew this was his only opportunity to find out whether what he'd experienced with her in the ballroom meant that she might want him as much as he wanted her.

He was filled with indecision, because to fall for a young officer and be on the verge of pursuing her was insane. At that thought, it appeared his integrity was stronger, and he watched her pale figure disappear into the dark.

Fuck this.

Jack leaned on the wooden railing. He knew that any chance he'd had of giving himself peace of mind and finding some resolution to the matter was fading. Despite that, he remained rooted there, as though he was tied there by invisible chains of duty and obligations.

He couldn't stop himself from watching her disappear from his sight and a string of expletives he would never have used in public burst from him. He was not in the least concerned that he might be overheard, and he clasped his hands together and stared at the shadowy sand piled against the supports below the deck.

The situation he found himself in was far from normal and the profanity allowed him to give vent to his frustration. He might not feel so pissed off and he could go back to doing what he did best—command the *BIA* without interference from emotional conflict.

Jack breathed in the potent brine-laden air and tried to relax before he returned to the ballroom. It was a struggle, but a few moments later he felt calmer, and he straightened and started to walk toward the double doors.

He'd nearly reached them when he heard a distant scream. He froze and looked over his shoulder. Lights from the hotel threw pools of gold onto the sand for approximately twenty feet and moonlight stippled the water's edge creating a pathway out to sea.

Sarah was nowhere to be seen, either in the immediate vicinity or in the distance.

It *had* been her and he sensed she was in trouble. He didn't know *how* he knew, but he was certain he needed to go to her. He strode back to the steps, descended the first two then jumped and cleared the rest before he jogged across the boardwalk.

Once he hit the beach, he picked up speed and ran in the direction of the flat, damp sand, toward where he thought the cry had originated. He kept up his pace, following the glinting surf on his right, his keen eyes searching his environment.

Even though he was alert for movement from someone or something who could have made what had sounded like a cry for help, he could see nothing. He might as well have been in a stygian, abandoned desert.

Jack continued to run. As he increased his distance from the hotel, there was still no sign of Sarah — if it had ever been her in the first place — and anxiety seized his gut.

He tried to regulate his breathing — made rapid with concern for her — by drawing air deep into his lungs and letting it out slowly. At last, his heartbeat became regular enough that the fear-induced adrenaline began to dissipate.

His gaze searched the gloom for a sign of her and finally he saw two figures off to his left. He immediately moderated his stride to a fast walk, still breathing easy from his enforced exercise, glad he'd maintained a strict fitness regime.

Pretty good for an old man.

He approached the couple and confirmed it was Sarah by the way her dress shimmered in the shifting shadows. His concern ramped up when he noticed she was kneeling on the sand with a man bending over her. Anger welled up inside him — overruling the worry — and he spiraled into a rage.

Jack clenched his hands into fists and slowed his pace even further. Moving with stealth, he altered his course to try and come up on Sarah's assailant from behind without alerting him to his presence. His white uniform was going to stand out like a beacon in the moonlight, but there was no alternative.

Using caution and covertness was the only strategy he had. He didn't want Sarah to get hurt in the scuffle which would undoubtedly result when he got his hands on the bastard who was hurting her.

He half-crouched and inched forward, crab-walking heel to toe to avoid his footfalls making any noise. He was rewarded when Sarah and her attacker remained oblivious to his approach.

Jack moved to within a few feet of the stranger and could make out Sarah's whimpered pleas. He saw that a length of her hair was wrapped around the man's hand and was being used as a rope to keep her in place. His rage became like a living thing inside him.

He'd always had a temper, evidenced by how many fights he'd had in school, but since being in the Navy, he'd learned how to control it. In the later years, he'd not been so quick to anger, because he believed in using harsh words as put-downs to avoid physical confrontations.

He would rather walk away before a situation escalated. However, at that moment, if the saying was true of someone seeing *red*, then Jack fit the bill.

He felt an incredible urge to beat the man to a pulp for daring to touch Sarah. He intended to kick the shit out of him then drag him to the water's edge and hold his head beneath the surface until he drowned.

Jack dug his nails into his palms to try to distract himself from his violent thoughts. He didn't have an opportunity to see if it had worked, because when he heard Sarah cry out in pain, he snapped.

He moved fast to cover the remaining distance between them, his cap tumbling to the sand. When he was close enough, he lunged forward and looped his arm around the man's neck to capture him in a head lock. He grasped the wrist of the hand that held Sarah's hair with his other and twisted the joint into a position it had never been meant to go in.

His quiet approach had been successful, because the stranger grunted in surprise, staggered backward and dragged Sarah with him. She over-balanced onto all fours, Jack heard her moan and she clutched her head. The sound ripped at his gut and fury blazed through his body.

He tried to mangle the attacker's limb, even break it so he would let her go. He must have succeeded, because the man howled like a wild animal and released her. Sarah fell forward onto the ground and, as soon as he'd let her go, Jack grasped his jacket collar, spun him and threw him onto the sand.

The assailant landed hard and Jack said in a voice filled with quiet menace, "I oughta beat the living shit outta you."

The man lay still then struggled to his feet. He weaved slightly, remained upright then hunched over, his injured hand cradled by the other. His face twisted with hate. "Well, well... The bitch's knight in shining armor has come to her rescue," he said.

Jack wasn't interested in the assaulter's aggressive demeanor. He thought it was nothing but an ill-conceived bravado. He stepped toward him and said, "Shut your mouth. Otherwise you'll wish you'd never been born."

The man staggered backward then stopped, stood his ground, and a grin split his shadowed features.

"You want the little slut. Is that it? Well, why didn't you say so, Navy man? I'll give her to you. I don't like sharing anyhow. She's not much...too whiny for my taste. I like them a bit more submissive."

Jack growled like an animal. "You don't know when to shut the fuck up, do you? You should have run while you could."

He took a single step forward and punched the man in the jaw. There was a faint crack and the assailant reeled sideways. He shook his head at the blow before he straightened and swung a fist at Jack's face. His knuckles clipped him above his right eyebrow.

The blow made Jack's head buzz for a moment, but he ignored the dull ringing in his ears and the throbbing that settled in his eye socket, and he grabbed the man by the throat.

A diaphanous red curtain fell over his vision and the world around him started to fade. He burrowed his fingers into the man's skin and muscle, curving their tips under cartilage and the hyoid bone in his throat with enough pressure to crack it and tear it out. His thumb pushed on the man's larynx to stop oxygen from getting into his lungs so he would suffocate.

Beyond reason, he slowly increased the pressure until he heard Sarah say in a trembling voice, "Sir. *Captain Chalmers*. Stop. You'll kill him."

Jack wanted to finish the vagrant off, but after she'd spoken, reason dispelled the fog in his brain. With a final crushing spasm of his hand, he loosened his iron grip and let the man go.

The perpetrator bent forward, wheezing and holding his throat. All the fight seemed to drain from his body and he sagged to his knees.

Jack twisted his lips in a grimace. "Go on. Beat it. I'll let the police can your sorry ass. If I ever see you again, I'll finish the job. Worthless motherfucker."

The stranger rose clumsily to his feet, straightened and ran, his lanky figure disappearing into the darkness that shielded the sand dunes.

Jack put his fisted hands on his hips, inhaled then exhaled slowly. He watched the man disappear into the night and picked up his cap. He dusted sand from the braid and insignia, put it on, then turned to where Sarah still knelt on the ground.

Still annoyed over what had happened, he glanced at the star-spangled sky, swore and went to her. Once he reached her side, he crouched and stared at her in silence.

Sarah raised her face to his and his heart ached to see the expression of anguish and hurt there. Anger coursed through his veins once more as he thought about the piece of scum who'd laid his filthy hands on her.

An impulse to take her in his arms and comfort her was strong. When he saw tears shimmer in her eyes, he almost gave in to the desire and had to restrain himself.

Instead, he asked softly, "Are you okay?"

Chapter Nine

Sarah felt sick to her stomach. Unnerved by the attack but surprised at Jack Chalmers' timely appearance, she wondered if she was in a nightmare. Everything seemed surreal and she shook her head to clear it then stared wide-eyed at the man before her.

His face was cast in shadow by the peak of his cap and his uniform glowed snow-white in the bright moonlight. With his pale hair, he looked like a ghost, and she shut her eyes for a few moments then opened them to see if he was still in front of her.

Jack's image remained and his presence confirmed that she *was* awake. To substantiate the fact, she touched her scalp and it hurt like hell.

She winced. "I'm sure the bastard tore out a chunk of my hair," she said, her voice quivering.

Jack rose, leaned forward and held out his hand. "Let's get you up."

Sarah slipped her palm into his and he closed his fingers around hers and pulled her to her feet. Once she'd regained her balance and had steadied herself, he released her.

"Are you sure you're okay?" he asked.

Sarah sighed. "My dress is ruined. A small fortune destroyed."

"It's easy enough to replace. A dress is a small price to pay for your life."

It was too dark for Sarah to make out his expression but she detected concern in his tone and something else she couldn't put her finger on.

"We should call the cops," she said.

Jack hesitated before he answered her, "I'm only going to because the bastard can't be allowed to get away with what he did. But, remember, Lieutenant. You were out here alone. The creep will be long gone and I took matters into my own hands and sucker-punched the son of a bitch. It's a recipe for a disaster. We could both be in a whole world of hurt and it won't look good on your record. Not only that, but we could be held in port until the investigation is over."

"I get that, but what happens if he does it to someone else?"

"I'm sure another woman wouldn't be so careless as to choose to walk on a deserted beach in the dark alone." Jack took a cell phone from his pants pocket and tapped out a number on the touch screen. Sarah listened as he asked for the police department, watched him as he was connected and heard him give a lengthy explanation as to what had happened.

He terminated the call and she heard irritation in his voice when he said, "They'll be here in ten mikes. We have to wait here for them."

Sarah glanced at his face and saw the expression of anger there. Uncomfortable at the trouble she'd caused, she said, "I'm sorry about this, sir. I should've used my common sense and been more responsible."

Jack folded his arms. "Yeah, Lieutenant, you should have. It's too late now, though. Let's deal with it and get out of here."

Sarah winced at the impatience in his voice. She didn't speak to him again but stared out to sea — very aware of him standing behind her — and wished the whole incident hadn't happened.

A few minutes later, she heard him say, "They're here."

She half-turned and her gaze followed his pointed finger to where blue lights flashed in the parking lot adjacent to the hotel.

Moments later, two dark figures appeared on the beach and jogged toward them. As they drew near, Sarah identified them as a male and female police officer.

Jack went to meet them and Sarah followed. Her face burned from embarrassment and she wished the night would end so she could go to her room and bury herself in sleep.

She and Jack were detained while she gave the female police officer a detailed description of the perpetrator and the officers took statements from both of them.

After she'd spoken about the matter, she was advised that there'd been another report made two days before in relation to an identical attack by a man resembling Sarah's assailant, a short distance from where they were.

She was filled with relief when she was reassured that based on both reports, there was a very good chance the man would be apprehended. Once he was, he would no longer pose a threat to her or anyone else. That was all that mattered.

The two officers left and Jack immediately turned to Sarah. "Why were you out here anyway?"

Sarah cringed at the harsh tone of his voice and ignored him. Instead, she concentrated on removing some of the now-dry sand from her dress.

At her lack of response Jack said, "Well?"

Sarah cleared her throat. "I…needed some fresh air. I didn't expect to be attacked by a psychopath."

"Big mistake, Lieutenant. You should have been more careful. A female out here by herself is asking for trouble."

Sarah frowned. "I don't think it's standard policy to expect a maniac to be stalking a public place a short distance from a hotel. It was hardly my fault he decided to choose the same night as me to do his thing. Pardon me for not agreeing with your view of things… Captain."

Jack ignored her heated words. "I'll take you back to the hotel and you can get yourself checked out."

Sarah was annoyed that he'd tried and convicted her without hearing her side of the story. It appeared he'd already decided she'd instigated the situation. Even if she were culpable, he could've been more diplomatic and sensitive about it.

"That's not necessary, sir. I can make my own way back," she replied. She slapped at the skirt of her dress to try to remove more sand.

"Negative, Morgan. Bad idea. The man might still be in the area. His type won't give up so easily. Follow me."

Jack began to walk toward the hotel, but Sarah hesitated. She hated the way he'd ordered her to accompany him and had strode off, assuming she would do so without argument. Stubbornness forced her to remain where she was.

Who in the hell does he think he is? Shit. What a stupid question.

Sarah decided common sense was better than stupidity, and once she'd found her sandals and her bag, she followed in the captain's wake like a disobedient child who'd been told off by her parents.

She caught up with him and drew alongside. Silence reigned between them, and she peeked at him and wondered what he was thinking. His good opinion meant a lot to her and she hoped he hadn't gotten the impression that she'd been stupid and reckless.

Approximately fifty feet from the hotel, where lights from its windows and the Deck Room spilled out onto the ochre-colored sand, Sarah stepped in front of Jack, causing him to stop.

He narrowed his eyes but ignored his obvious irritation and studied his face to confirm what she'd noticed earlier.

There was a wound over his right eye, and although it was only approximately half an inch in length, it was deep and blood had trickled down his jaw to his chin. It had obviously been caused when her attacker had kicked off and swung a punch at him.

"You're injured," she said.

Jack shrugged. "It's no big deal. It doesn't hurt. I'll get it fixed at the hotel," he said.

"Yeah, and the crew will have a field day if they see you. I'll take you back to my room."

Jack raised an eyebrow and his mouth twitched, as though he was going to smile. It quickly disappeared and he said, "No go, Lieutenant. It'll look mighty odd to the natives if I'm seen sneaking into one of my crew's accommodations."

Sarah frowned, unsure what he meant, then remembered what she'd said and snorted. "Get over yourself. I meant I have a first-aid kit in my room and I can treat you there. I didn't mean I was going to try to get into your pants."

She thought of how she'd phrased her words and how insubordinate she might have sounded and groaned inwardly.

How many more inches deep am I going to dig this hole for myself?

She bowed her head and waited for the dressing-down she was sure she was going to receive about how to speak to and treat an officer.

Instead, Jack cleared his throat. "Since you put it like that, Lieutenant, lead on. I take it you *have* got a plan for *sneaking* me in the back way."

Still irritated with him but also exasperated with herself for not thinking before she spoke, Sarah wanted to ignore his question. She wasn't about to complicate matters further, though, and replied, "There's a side entrance with an elevator. I'm on the second floor and, as everyone will be as drunk as a skunk and nobody should see us, your virtue should be quite safe."

She thought she heard the man chuckle, but when she looked at him to see if she'd guessed right, his face was expressionless. He gestured with his hand for her to precede him, and without wasting any more time, she led the way from the deck area to the hotel.

They didn't speak to one another as they left the beach. Sarah led him to a small door that she'd discovered offered much easier access and egress from the hotel if a person wanted to avoid other guests and the crowded bars and restaurants inside.

When they reached the entrance, she stopped and Jack halted behind her, his arm brushing hers. His touch stirred her senses and she closed her eyes briefly then lifted the push bar.

As had been the case on the previous occasion she'd used the door, it was unlocked, so she shoved it open to reveal a short corridor, empty but for the steel frame of an elevator.

She and Jack went inside and she pressed a single button on the wall to call the car. The air was heavy with tension and she stared with intense concentration at the numbers, each one highlighting in red, showing the lift descending floor by floor.

On its arrival, the doors slid open with a ping and Jack stepped aside to allow her to enter first before he followed her in. Sarah stabbed at a button marked 'two' with a trembling finger and stood almost at attention while the automatic doors shut and the elevator ascended.

By the time they reached her floor, she was torn with regret that she'd offered to give him first aid at all. She wanted to scream to break the tense atmosphere which had built to an unbearable level between them, and she gritted her teeth.

The elevator came to a stop and she hurried out into the hallway, hoping Jack would follow behind her. She wanted to get rid of him, end the night and be alone with her thoughts.

Sarah's bare feet scuffed on the luxurious carpet, accompanied by the faint thud of Jack's footsteps as they walked along the corridor. As they approached her room, she withdrew a blue plastic key card from her purse and swiped it through the magnetic machine above the handle.

The door opened with a click and she pushed on it and stepped aside so Jack could go ahead of her into the room.

This is such a bad idea. I've now got him in my room and God knows what's going to happen next.

Sarah stepped through the doorway and dropped her sandals to the floor. She debated whether she should leave the door ajar. Contrary to her mixed emotions, she pushed it shut, effectively sealing herself inside a room with the man whom she'd thought about for months.

She'd left a lamp on before going to the ball and a soft golden glow bathed the bed but left the rest of the room in shadows. She searched her surroundings, making sure she hadn't left any lingerie lying around. She sighed with relief when she saw there was nothing in sight that might have embarrassed them both.

She half-turned to the man beside her and gestured toward a chair in the corner. "Why don't you make yourself comfortable over there and I'll get the medical kit."

Without waiting to see if he complied, Sarah went to her sea bag and unzipped it. She delved into its depths and pulled out a small white box before she straightened. She lifted a plastic cup from a shelf over the sink and filled it with hot water before she tested the temperature, found it too hot and cooled it with cold.

She carried the water and the container to where Jack had seated himself on an elegant, spindle-legged seat and tried not to smile when she saw how uncomfortable he looked balanced there, as if he were concerned it might collapse beneath his weight.

She knelt in front of him and placed everything on the floor beside her. An idea popped into her mind that in any other circumstances, her kneeling position might appear both submissive and provocative.

Sarah nibbled her bottom lip to distract her thoughts and opened the medical supplies. Her attention turned to Jack and her heart skipped a beat. He was bending forward, his elbows resting on his thighs, his big hands clasped between his legs. He was staring at her with a veiled expression.

His gaze made her stomach turn somersaults. She wished he would show some other expression than the inscrutable one which seemed part of his general demeanor. The only thing that showed he might be experiencing emotion was the flicker of a muscle in his jaw.

Why's he staring at me like that?

He was still wearing his cap, and Sarah gestured to it with her hand and said with a tremble in her voice, "I'll…have to take this off so I can see to your cut."

Jack stayed quiet. While she was reluctant to perform such a personal act, she took his silence as consent, grasped the peak with her thumb and forefinger, took the headgear off and placed it on the carpet beside the chair.

She squirmed beneath his gaze, cleared her throat and said, "Let's get this wound seen to, sir, then you can get out of here."

"Yeah. Let's do that."

Jack's tone was curt. She glanced at him once more then turned to the kit set out beside her.

Sarah hoped her hands would stay steady and not disclose how nervous and on edge she was at being so close to him. She selected some cotton-wool balls, soaked them in the water then squeezed the moisture out and leaned toward him.

She saw the area around the wound was beginning to swell and she gently cleaned his face before she dealt with the laceration.

"I won't touch the cut. The blood has clotted and I don't want it to start bleeding again."

Jack remained uncommunicative, and when she looked at him once more, she discovered that in the time she'd attended to his injury, she'd moved her own face closer to his.

Their gazes locked and she was held captive. He studied her with what appeared to be a probing visual caress and Sarah suddenly found it hard to breathe. It was as if the oxygen content in the room had decreased while her body temperature had risen dramatically.

She sat back on her heels and dropped the bloody cotton wool into the cup. She found a piece of gauze, dried his face then dabbed at the gash. Once she'd finished, she took some skin-closing Steri-Strip from its sterile packet and placed it vertically across the laceration, effectively holding the wound together.

"There you are, sir. You're good to go."

Sarah wanted to get as far away from him as she could. She was about to get to her feet when, without warning, Jack Chalmers leaned in to her even farther and cupped her face in his palms, causing her to utter a squeak of surprise.

"I've wanted to do this for so long," he said.

Chapter Ten

Jack's lips brushed Sarah's, light and tender. His hands were warm on her face and the movement of his lips on hers made her want to melt into him.

Her defenses began to crumble.

Defenses? What defenses?

Her whole world narrowed until it was just the two of them. The kiss continued and her desire for him consumed her, beginning to swallow everything that she'd considered normal before his lips had touched hers.

In a part of her mind where the unfulfilled erotic side of her nature stirred, she wanted him more than she'd ever wanted another man. He'd taken command of her mouth and aroused sensations in her body. She had to use all her self-control to stop herself from kissing him harder.

Her resistance was disintegrating fast. She no longer had the willpower to stop — and didn't want to. A small voice whispered a warning in her mind, but it was too late. She dismissed the mental admonition as being of no consequence.

Sarah lifted her hand and rested her palm on the side of his face. Stubble rasped under her fingertips, and she trailed them along his jawline and felt the faint flicker of a muscle beneath his skin.

Jack parted her lips with his tongue and his breathing quickened. She wanted to dissolve into him but fear that she might show her true feelings stopped her. Besides, his palms on her face kept them apart, so she closed her eyes, slid her hands to the back of his neck and stroked his skin.

He slid a hand to the base of her skull and clenched his fingers in her hair, then he relaxed them and gently caressed the back of her head.

With a demanding increase in pressure, he pulled Sarah's head forward until his mouth was hard on hers. Their kiss deepened, her desire burned like fire and she became lost in the feelings that were taking control of her.

Sarah glided her fingers from his neck and meshed them in his short hair. He shivered at her touch, and at his response, she suddenly wanted much more than a mere kiss from him and would have given him anything if he'd asked.

She was therefore shocked when, a few seconds later, Jack broke away from her.

"I apologize, Lieutenant," he said. "That should never have happened. I was way out of line."

Sarah's heart raced, and she raised a hand to her mouth and traced her lips with trembling fingers.

A few moments later, his words scattered her chaotic thoughts and penetrated the mist of sexual passion which had fogged her senses. Their kiss had opened the floodgates and the pent-up emotions she'd kept hidden from him were exposed. She wanted — no — *needed* an explanation.

She stared at him in confusion. "Why shouldn't it have happened?" she asked.

Jack's voice was emotionless and stilted when he replied, "We can't do this. US Navy Regulation 1165 — "

Sarah interrupted him, her tone flat. "Prohibits personal relationships between officers and enlisted personnel that are unduly familiar and do not respect the differences in grade or rank. I've read the rules as well."

Jack continued relentlessly, "Here's another one then. No person in the Navy shall enter into a relationship that does not respect differences in rank and is prejudicial to good order and discipline."

A few minutes prior to his withdrawal from her, the pulsating longing for him had been overwhelming. Now all Sarah wanted to do was cry.

"Why?" she asked.

"Why what?"

"Why does it have to be like that?"

Jack ran his fingers through his hair. His words were curt when he said, "It has to. If it were allowed, it would affect morale and the combat readiness of the ship. I can't let that happen."

Sarah frowned then shook her head. "Please don't quote the rule book to me, Jack."

Jack stared at her with what looked to be tactical intent. He became still and quiet.

The silence stretched between them and grew awkward. She couldn't understand how everything could have gone so drastically wrong.

To break the hush, she said, "This is not the time for throwing differences in our rank around or trying to figure out the meaning behind 'unduly familiar' or 'fraternization'. I know there are important issues at stake here, but you can't just kiss me and expect me to ignore it. You owe me an explanation." Sarah drew in a deep breath and continued, "You're not interested in me. Is that it?"

"You're kidding, right?" Jack said in a cold voice. "Do I act like I'm not interested? You've got no idea, have you, Sarah?"

Sarah almost smiled when he stopped speaking. Emboldened and shameless, the urge to touch him almost irresistible, Sarah crawled forward until she was positioned between his knees.

She gazed at him, the mask she'd worn to keep her emotions hidden from him banished. "Well?" she asked. "Where do we go from here?"

Jack ran his fingers through his hair again. He took both her hands in his, his thumbs kneading her palms, sending tingles along her skin. "We aren't going to go anywhere, Sarah. We can't. We mustn't."

He shook his head then bowed it before he lifted his gaze to meet hers once more. "I care for you…a lot, too much to let this situation go any further. And I think you know it's the right thing to do."

Sarah wanted to withdraw her hands from his grasp but she needed to feel his touch. It kept her grounded, because her world was crashing around her and she felt him slipping away from her.

"You don't know what I think or how I feel," she said.

Jack stroked her palms as if he sensed she was about to pull away. "You're not stupid. There's too much at stake for us to get into a relationship."

"No, Jack. There's something else. How can you deny your — *our* feelings — for the sake of damn rules and regulations?"

Sarah had no intention of letting him go. She needed to know whether he had the same feelings for her as she had for him. She was going to try her hardest to get him to admit *something* so they could move on, whether it was forward or backward.

"You don't give a guy a chance, do you? You just wade in with guns blazing."

Sarah lifted her chin. "That's not in my resume. You should know. You seem to have *read* my personal file."

Jack let go of her and folded his arms. The planes of his face had gone hard and his eyes were angry, as though her words had insulted his sense of ethics.

Sarah lowered her gaze, the skin of her hands still tingling, and she heard him sigh. When he finally spoke, his tone was hesitant. "What about the age gap, Sarah? How old are you? Twenty-four? Twenty-five? I must be eighteen years older than you. Let's put aside the small issue of getting our asses kicked if we were found out. Do you honestly want to be with a man who's close to middle-age and acts like he has a poker up his ass?"

Sarah heard the raw emotion in his voice and she searched his face. The impassive expression had vanished, replaced by one of regret, and when she saw it, she weakened but stayed silent, waiting.

Jack growled with what sounded like frustration. "Gimme a break, will you?"

Sarah put a hand on each knee and slid her palms up his thighs.

"Sarah," Jack said, a warning in his voice.

Despite the censure in his tone, his powerful muscles flinched at her touch and her spirits soared at his obvious response.

In for a penny, in for a pound. I've thrown myself at him and now I've got nothing to lose by confessing everything.

"I don't give a damn about the age difference. Ever since I've been aboard the *BIA*, I've been…attracted to you, although that's too simple a word to describe my feelings. I've never wanted anyone else. I have no idea what will happen with us or even if there is an us, because I didn't plan any of this. I want *you*, Jack. It's not about me being on a status trip because it'd be great to get involved with my commanding officer so he can help me climb the promotion ladder. To me you're just an ordinary man, so please, don't ask me to defend what I feel for you. Can we now lay the age issue to rest?"

Jack stared at her his expression resolute. "Uh-huh. Are you always this bossy and demanding?"

"Yeah. Get used to it."

Sarah detected the reluctance in his demeanor and was devastated to think she might have lost whatever tenuous grip she'd had on the situation. She was silent for a moment, then said, "I understand where you're coming from, Jack. I do. I don't know what you must think of me right now. I've thrown myself at you, but please believe me when I say I've never done it before. It's certainly not something I would do with anyone else…except you. I think I've pushed you and I'm sorry. I wouldn't have said anything if I hadn't thought…"

Her voice trailed off into silence and she blushed, feeling humiliated. She'd acted with boldness and temerity toward someone who was out of bounds and not in her league, and she had lost the battle. She was tired and wanted it to be over.

Abruptly, Jack pushed his chair backward and got to his feet. Sarah steadied herself then tensed. She thought he was going to leave and was surprised when instead he leaned forward, took her hand in his and drew her to her feet.

Once she was standing, he placed a hand on either side of her waist.

"Come here," he ordered and pulled her in tight to him.

"You're quite a handful, you know that?" he said, his breath warm on her ear.

For a moment, Sarah hesitated, then she entwined her arms about his neck. His body pressed into hers and he slid his hands around to her back then tightened his grip until she could barely draw oxygen into her lungs.

Their mouths were only inches apart and, with a sensual yearning that made her senses reel, she wanted him to kiss her again.

Chapter Eleven

"You've made me crazy over the last few months,"
Jack said. "Onboard ship, when I was near you, all I
wanted to do was talk to you and touch you like any
normal guy—and I couldn't. I didn't know what the
hell to do with myself. I've lost count of how many
times I almost ordered you to come to my quarters so I
could be alone with you."

Delight flooded through Sarah at his words. She
touched his face with her fingertips then trailed them
along his jawline. "Each time I walked past your
quarters, I had to stop myself from knocking on your
door," she said. "I used to think up reasons for being
there, but they were so obvious. I even checked the
watch roster to try to work out when you weren't on
duty. The problem was that I never knew if someone
might've been with you. I think it would've been
damned clear why I was there. I could've gotten both
of us in trouble, including having you court martial me
for stalking a ranking officer."

Jack grinned and kissed her forehead. "Oh, I think I could've come up with a plausible explanation for you being there."

He cupped her chin with his hand and his mouth met hers. He kissed her with a raw and intense passion, and a wave of heat spread through Sarah's body. Their tongues entwined and she flattened her palms on the back of his head to pull him toward her.

He tugged her to bring her in close to him and his erection pressed against her lower belly. She rotated her hips to create a delicious friction and heard his sharp intake of breath.

He bucked his pelvis in response, then he moved from her mouth to kiss her neck and her naked collarbone. Tingles raced down her spine and Sarah moaned then licked and nipped the delicate area under his ear.

Jack put his hand on her waist then skimmed his hand up her spine. He stopped at her neck to stroke the skin there before he glided both his palms downward to clasp her bottom.

He pulled her even closer so her hips were crushed to his. She squirmed at the exquisite pressure building between her thighs, the sensation causing her to almost lose the strength in her legs.

She clung to him and Jack grazed her cheek with his lips before he trailed small kisses along her neck once more. "You smell so good," he whispered.

Sarah could only moan in response, because desire had rendered her speechless. The only thoughts that made any sense to her were centered on how he was touching her and the sensations engulfing her.

The smell of his cologne teased her nose. She tasted him with her tongue then nipped his neck.

He rocked his groin against hers in a steady rhythm then gripped her hips and pulled her in to him — rough and hard — until his penis was crushed between them.

He tightened his grip on her backside then captured her lips and kissed her again hungrily.

The warmth of his mouth fanned the flames simmering inside her. She ached for him to take her. She craved his cock inside her and for him to plunge into her with deep, hard strokes and bring about her release.

Sarah panted in short, sharp gasps and kissed him harder. She thrust her tongue into his mouth, and at her silent urging, Jack's breathing grew harsh and uneven in synchronization with her own.

She slid her hands from behind his neck and skimmed her palms down his powerful arms, then upward and along his broad shoulders to his neck.

The intense burn of sexual excitement increased. The firestorm encompassing her body grew white-hot and she didn't know how long it would be before she demanded that he make love to her.

As if he sensed her need, Jack drew away from her. "Are you sure this is what you want, Sarah?" he asked, his voice hoarse.

Sarah kissed his mouth, licked his bottom lip then drew back. "I've never been so sure about anything in my life."

Jack growled low in his throat and picked her up. After a brief struggle with her long skirt, she hooked her legs around his hips and nestled her face into his shoulder. He moved toward the bed, where he set her on her feet then kissed her once more.

After only a few moments, he stopped the kiss and they stared at each other, her eyes searching his for any signs of doubt. Seeing only that he wanted her as much as she wanted him, Sarah wasted no time. She placed her palms flat on his chest then slowly slid them toward the topmost gold button of his tunic.

Jack watched her hands then lifted his gaze to her face. She undid the first fastening at his neck, her movements slow and languid, then went on to the next until they were all undone. She opened his jacket and stared at the sculptured landscape of his pectoral and stomach muscles.

They were clearly defined and finely honed, not showy but conveying that he was at the peak of fitness. She placed her hands on the smooth, tan skin of his ribs and ran her fingertips down his belly to the waistband of his pants.

Jack was silent and didn't move. Sarah glanced at him from beneath her eyelashes and noted that his jaw was tense and the color of his eyes had darkened. There was an expression in them that made her want to rub herself to relieve the burgeoning fullness and send her over the edge into orgasm.

With a sense of urgency, she pushed the tunic off his shoulders and tried to slide the sleeves down his arms. The material snagged on his contoured biceps and the garment stopped and wouldn't go any farther.

She cursed under her breath and Jack laughed out loud. He shrugged off the jacket, catching it before it fell to the floor and threw it over the unlit lamp on a bedside table.

An elaborate black tattoo of a hawk covered his left shoulder and bicep, and Sarah traced the intricate pattern with her finger. It rippled when he moved his arm and she licked the area then placed featherlight kisses on his skin while she grasped the waistband of his pants and pulled him closer.

Sarah massaged his stomach and his muscles flinched. When he clutched her to him, she stood on tiptoe and rotated her hips against his cock. She trailed her fingers along his ribs and marveled at the ripple of his muscles before she skimmed them slowly to his sides and curved them in across his belly.

He jerked his hips and grabbed her but she looked at him, smiled seductively and shook her head.

"Wait," she whispered.

She slid her fingers to the button of his pants and, taking her time, undid it and grasped the zip. He put his hand on top of hers and shook his head.

Jack reached behind her and drew the fastening of her dress to the waist of her skirt. As the beaded front fell away, exposing her to his heated gaze, cool air caressed Sarah's flushed skin. She waited anxiously for his reaction to her nakedness.

Jack stared at her full breasts with their erect nipples before he raised his gaze to her face again.

"You're beautiful," he said.

He grasped the dress and slid it down her legs until it lay in a green pool on the carpet.

Sarah rested a hand on his shoulder to steady herself and stepped out of it. Jack hooked his fingers in the thin elastic of her see-through gauzy panties and pulled them to her ankles. She kicked them aside and watched as he grabbed them and tossed the flimsy material into a corner of the room.

Jack's hot gaze settled on her body. His eyes scorched her as they raked her skin, and her pulse rate rocketed. He kicked off his shoes, unzipped his pants, pushed them to his ankles and, once he'd taken them off, threw them to join his tunic.

Sarah's gaze roamed his tan torso, which was dark against the brilliant white of his shorts, and came to rest on the outline of his penis that tented his underwear.

She traced his length with a finger and licked her bottom lip. Her whole body was hungry for him and she pulled the waistband away, freeing him.

Chapter Twelve

Jack picked Sarah up and laid her on the bed, where she fell backward and opened herself to him. He lowered himself between her legs and she encircled his hips and tensed her muscles to pull his pelvis toward her so that his cock nudged at her entrance.

His elbows, one on either side of her, supported his weight. She clasped his hands with her own and threaded her fingers through his. He pressed them to the mattress, his grip tight enough to almost crush her fragile bones.

His kiss was brief but hot and hard. He licked her lips sensually then left liquid-hot kisses, first on her face, then her jawline and at last her neck, where a pulse raced beneath her highly sensitized skin.

Shivers raced along her limbs and Sarah moaned then tilted her head into the soft comforter to give him the room he needed.

Jack traced her lips with his tongue then darted possessively into her mouth and pushed her into the mattress.

The kiss was searing and nearly blew her mind, and the fire in her blood consumed every thought she had. She whimpered with her need for him.

His penis was rock-hard proof as to how aroused he was and it throbbed against her thigh. She arched her back and tried to settle in on it. She was desperate for him and wanted him to enter her — to hell with foreplay — and make love to her...hard.

Jack left her mouth, bent his head and licked a nipple. Sarah squeezed his fingers in response and he circled the bud slowly with his tongue then took it into his mouth, sucking it until she writhed in pleasurable torment.

He left the erect nubbin and pressed gentle swirling kisses on the way to the other one. Exquisite sexual enjoyment coursed through Sarah. She needed him inside her and her body writhed at his ministrations. Jack laughed softly in an alpha male way.

He stared into her face. "In a hurry?" he asked, his mouth close to hers.

"Yes," Sarah answered, her voice husky with arousal. "I want you, Jack."

"I want you too," he responded.

His gaze returned to the hard buds of her nipples, as if he were determined to make them both wait. Sarah wanted to scream out for him to take her.

When he kissed each breast in turn, his teeth grazed the sensitive skin and she gasped at the assault.

She let go of his right hand and pushed her own between them to massage the rigid muscles of his stomach. She glided her fingers down to bury them in the thick hair that nestled his penis, and she slowly stroked the area for a few moments, then took his rigid cock in her hand.

She circled the bulging glans with the fleshy pad of her thumb and trailed a finger along the silken, smooth, engorged vein on the underside.

Jack thrust forward and back rhythmically and Sarah rocked her hips, countering him. His dick glided through her grip, pre-cum making her actions slick and molten.

Sarah tightened her hold on him. She slid her hand up and down until he clamped his hand over hers and stayed her movement.

He shook his head. "Don't…because I want you so damn bad."

A silken wetness coated her inner thighs and her cleft ached. She wanted Jack with a rough, bittersweet passion that only he could satisfy, and it took an enormous effort to stop herself from guiding him into her and losing herself in the erotic sensations he had introduced her to.

Jack released her other hand, grasped her hips and lifted her bottom off the bed before he thrust the engorged tip of his penis into her.

Sarah gasped. "Oh—" she said and opened herself to him, welcoming his forceful entrance.

She clenched her legs around his hips and he slipped in slow and deep. Her body jerked and her whole being became focused on that one point where their bodies joined—her, Jack, his cock and how perfectly they fit together. It was Jack, all Jack.

A kick of lust whipped Sarah into a frenzy, and as he filled her completely, she clenched her internal muscles around him. She tightened them again as he nearly pulled out of her, and she repeated her motions with each powerful thrust.

He stopped and held her gaze with his. "You want this?"

Jack moved his penis with compelling, teasing thrusts and she whimpered. "Yes, I want it...please."

Jack rotated his hips, his dick touching all around inside her and Sarah clawed at his sweating chest and bucked her hips, frantic for release.

Their lips met again in heated passion. He kissed her roughly and she thrust her hips forward, then he pulled back his cock until he was almost out of her.

For a few seconds she froze and he plunged back inside her, his stiff shaft plundering her delicate insides. The friction created an intense wave of pleasure at her core and she cried out, encouraging and urging him to take her over the edge.

Jack quickened his pace, and with deep and powerful strokes, he rocked against her clit. An incredible need ignited and consumed her, and she returned the movements smoothly and rapidly.

Her onrushing orgasm began to peak and spiral out of control and her moans grew louder. Their gazes locked and she sensed he was as close to his climax as she was to hers.

As if fueled by her moans of pleasure, Jack pounded into Sarah faster and harder. Her orgasm exploded, creating a whirlpool of intense sensation and such overwhelming pleasure that she wanted to scream.

She tensed, arched her spine and clung to his shoulders — to let go would be to allow both her mind and body to spiral into a vortex from which she might never want to return — every nerve on fire and her body quivering.

As her muscles clenched around his cock, Jack jerked his head back, uttered a guttural shout and rammed into her one final time before he came.

As he emptied himself into her, Sarah's heart thundered unevenly in her chest and she gasped for air. Jack released her hips and hugged her, and she kissed a tiny pulse that raced in his neck and rested her forehead at the base of his throat. His heart pounded fast in conjunction with her own, and she felt the diminishing throb of him inside her and wanted to stay in his arms always.

Chapter Thirteen

Jack entwined his fingers in Sarah's hair and pressed his mouth to hers, the kiss hard and hungry. Once more, she experienced the helplessness, the sinking yielding to him and the surging warmth that left her limp each time he touched her.

Her heart continued to race and she returned the kiss with all the feeling she had for him.

He became hard inside her once more, and she clenched the muscles at her core to draw him deep inside.

Jack pulled back from their kiss and brushed wispy tendrils from where they clung to her damp forehead.

He smiled and stared into her eyes. "Holy shit," he said softly.

Sarah's lips were bruised and swollen from his forceful kisses and she licked them to moisten them. "Is that a good 'holy shit' or a bad 'holy shit'?" she murmured, her voice hesitant.

Jack traced a thumb along her mouth and she kissed it before licking the tip. He jerked his hand away and a grin lifted the corner of his mouth. It was sexy as hell, like the man himself, and it captivated her.

"It's neither," he finally replied. "It's a *wow* 'holy shit'."

Her laugh was seductive. "So, I pass muster?" She lowered her gaze and stared at him from beneath her eyelashes.

Jack was silent for a moment. "More than you'll ever know."

A meaningful silence flowed between them, then his lips twisted in a grimace. "Sorry to destroy the moment, but shall we move up the bed? You must be uncomfortable."

Sarah shook her head. "I want to stay here all night," she replied, satiated contentment flowing through her body.

"I could as well, but I'm going to suffer a very embarrassing leg cramp and I don't want to be in this position when it happens, because I might hurt you."

Jack uttered a small groan of discomfort. He rolled off her and onto his back and began to knead the muscle in the upper part of his leg.

Eventually, he sighed with relief and turned onto his stomach before getting to his knees and moving to the opposite side of the bed.

Sarah eyed the way the muscles in his thighs and bottom flexed as he moved away from her and a primal lust flooded through her.

You are seriously insatiable when it comes to this man.

Jack's voice interrupted her thoughts and he beckoned to her with a finger. "C'mere."

Sarah joined him and lay beside him. She moved close to him, and when he put his arm around her, she nestled against his body, his skin touching hers.

She pressed herself to him, enticing him for more sex, and Jack kissed her forehead.

"You're a surprise, Sarah," he said quietly.

Sarah closed her eyes, "I am?" she said. "What makes you say that?"

Jack was silent for a moment. "I had no idea you felt anything for me."

Sarah opened her eyes and looked at him. "Like, how could you know? I never let on, and you had more than enough to contend with on the *BIA*. Anyway, I couldn't have told you, even if I'd wanted to."

"It's not going to be easy, Sarah," Jack went on. "When we're on the ship, we're going to have to keep as far away from each other as possible in case somebody suspects. I wouldn't want to jeopardize our jobs. If someone finds out about us, it'll be a damn sight more than a board of inquiry or being stripped of our ranks."

Sarah rubbed his chest. "Your job is important, Jack. I won't cause any trouble for you. You've got far more to lose than I have." She smiled seductively. "I'm certainly not going to turn up in your quarters in the middle of the night in my sexiest underwear to seduce you when we're off duty...no matter how much I might want to."

Jack frowned. "Why the hell not? I think I'll hold on to that thought for later. It'll be something for me to think about during those long, lonely hours without you."

Sarah trailed a finger from his chest to where the sheet lay on his stomach below his navel, and ran the tip along his abdomen.

Jack squirmed. "Stop that, unless you want to follow it up with something else."

Sarah smiled to herself. "Such as? Have you got something in mind?"

"Oh, yeah. Plenty."

"Yes, well. I've got to use the restroom. Close your eyes."

Jack frowned. "What the hell for?"

"I'm not going to the bathroom with you staring at me."

Jack laughed out loud. "Are you kidding me? I've seen your naked body—and stunning it is, I might add—and after everything we've done, I'm not allowed to look at you?"

Sarah sat up and covered her breasts with the sheet. "Shut them, buddy. Last word on the matter."

Jack sighed but obeyed and Sarah rose and ran for the washroom. She quickly pushed the door open, stepped inside and fumbled for the light switch.

Before she closed it, she peeked over her shoulder at Jack and smiled because he was still doing what she'd told him to do.

She took care of her business and flushed the toilet then, while she washed her hands, she stared into a large mirror that hung on the wall over the sink.

"Oh, hell," she whispered. "I look a mess."

Her hair was tangled as though someone had run their fingers through it.

He has.

Her eyes were smeared with the remains of her makeup and were heavy-lidded. Her chin was a faint pink where Jack's stubble had inflamed the sensitive skin there. Her lips were swollen and she ran a finger along them. A thrill coursed through her when she remembered he'd caused it through his forceful kisses.

"Hey, are you okay in there? I'm getting kinda lonesome."

Sarah laughed when she heard Jack's voice. "Patience is obviously not one of your virtues," she said.

She grabbed a handful of toilet tissue from the roll, soaked the bundle under the hot water and hurriedly cleaned away the remnants of mascara and eyeliner. She flushed the whole lot down the toilet then, eager to get back to his side, she opened the door and stepped into the room.

Jack was sitting up, his eyes open, his gaze focused on her, and she stopped.

Her face flushed and her nipples hardened at the look of desire on his face. "Cheat," she exclaimed.

"Very nice," he said and drew back the covers. "Now, back to your post, ma'am."

Sarah laughed and hurried to the bed. She climbed in beside him, and after he'd settled against the headboard, she cuddled into him and rested her palm on his stomach.

Silence fell between them and Sarah wondered if he'd fallen asleep.

She trailed two fingers from his lower ribs to the sheet that once more covered his groin and inserted the tip beneath the cotton. She glided it downward until she touched the thick hair that surrounded his penis.

He uttered a sound and jerked his hips toward her questing digits.

"What are you doing?" he asked, now clearly wide awake.

"Why don't you guess?" Sarah replied, inching lower until she felt his hot hardness.

Jack cleared his throat. "Why don't you tell me?"

"Well…" Sarah paused, lowered her voice and said, "I'm going to take your cock in my hand and get you really hard. Then, I'm going to take you in my mouth and —"

"All stop," Jack said, his voice hoarse. "The first part of your…plan has been successful."

Sarah pretended to be disappointed. "Oh, what a shame. Do you want me to stop what I'm doing then?"

She gently massaged him and teased his groin with her fingertips.

"Fuck no. Don't you dare."

Sarah gave him a chaste kiss on the mouth before she bit his neck gently. He tightened his arm about her shoulders and moaned.

"Are you okay?" she asked when she drew back, knowing full well he wasn't.

Jack grasped a skein of her hair and tugged on it. "Nope. With you around, I'm never going to be okay again."

Chapter Fourteen

Jack pushed Sarah onto her back and kissed her. She sucked his tongue when he thrust it into her mouth, then she put her arms around him. She pressed her palms to the smooth skin of his back and felt the power in his muscles when he moved.

He prodded her with his cock and she turned her body toward his and rotated her hips in small circles so her groin rubbed his.

Jack trailed his fingers from her stomach to her left breast. He glided his palm over its curve and her nipples tightened into rigid nubs in response.

Sarah gasped when he pinched and pulled at an erect bud then circled it with his thumb. She raised herself to kiss him but Jack kept her where she was, leaned over her and licked the highly sensitive area.

His tongue laved her nipple before he took it into his mouth, and Sarah, while wanting him to remain there, rested a hand on top of his to stop him from going any farther.

Jack raised his head. "What's wrong?" he asked.

Sarah didn't answer. Instead, she pushed him until he rolled away from her and lay flat, then she raised herself and leaned over him. She ran her eyes along his body and kissed his chest, his muscles twitching at her touch.

A primeval excitement coursed through her when she thought of the power she possessed to turn him on so much. She placed the palm of her hand on his stomach and raised her head to watch him.

Jack's gaze was molten, and she slowly and sensually moistened her lips with her tongue. She lowered her head and trailed it along to his nipple where she licked it then nipped at his skin.

When she stared at him once more, the expression on his face was one she understood well, because it showed the want and need that she felt for him.

Jack stayed motionless while she kissed his eyes, his mouth, his jaw and his collarbone. She placed featherlight kisses, one on each nipple, interspersing them with delicate nips and swirling licks and, at last, he groaned in response.

She retraced her movements to his shoulder, kissed his tattoo and worked her way around his ribcage before returning to his nipples, swiping them with her tongue and nibbling them in one place then another.

With her other hand, she slid her fingertips to his chest then his stomach, running them lower and slower until she touched his groin.

His erection was rigid. She trailed her fingers along his cock and circled the crown then raised herself to her knees and kissed his stomach.

Her body made whispering sounds on the linen as she moved downward, tracing her tongue and lips along his body in a slow and seductive crawl, teasing the tan skin of his stomach. She kissed his lower belly and he pushed his hips at her, as if in anticipation of what she was going to do next.

She bit his stomach gently then kissed one hip bone followed by the other. Then she raised her head. "Do you want me to stop?" she asked, deliberately teasing him.

Jack's voice was a hoarse whisper when he said, "Me? Nope."

Her nipples ached with unfulfillment and her juices wet her cleft and inner thighs with her own heightened sexual desire. She was wet and ready for him again.

She grasped the sheet and tossed it to his knees. His cock reared from its nest of hair and she rested her hand on the hot, silken skin and grasped him firmly. He throbbed in her palm and she squeezed him and moved her hand up and down. His growl sent heat pooling between her legs.

"I'm so glad," she said and trailed her tongue across his stomach, from one side to the other. "Otherwise" — she kissed the glans of his cock—"we'd have to take a rain check and get some rest."

Jack uttered a guttural growl and arched his groin. His dick brushed her face. "You've got no chance of that, lady."

Sarah rubbed her cheek on the silken-smooth crown and squeezed his turgid, straining shaft. "I guess—"

She leaned over him once more and lowered her head. She paused, teasing him, then very slowly licked his penis, creating intricate circles along his skin until she took the glans in her mouth, sucked once and released him.

She was panting when she glanced at Jack again, loving and wanting to see his reaction to her ministrations. Once more, he was watching her and their gazes locked, the sexual tension between them heightening, each knowing what the other wanted and anticipating and savoring the outcome.

Sarah gave him a last wanton look then caressed his hot skin with the tip of her tongue . He bucked his hips to meet her mouth and his obvious need for her caused a deep and erotic craving to stir inside her.

Without pausing, Sarah gripped him and began to squeeze and release him intermittently. At the same time, she took his cock into her mouth and sucked gently, using her tongue to lash at his burgeoning shaft.

Jack's little moans and grunts excited her and she loved listening to them. She sucked hard and pumped him. With each pull of her mouth, she extended her reach, and he rested his hand on the back of her head and guided her on his dick. Sarah obliged by taking him deep into her mouth.

She tasted the faint salty tang of him, and the way he filled her mouth stirred a sensual carnality in her. She gently stroked his balls and cupped them in her palm, marveling at how tight they'd become.

Jack's breathing sped up and his groans increased. "Holy. Fucking. Shit," he said and he moved his hips hard, signaling that he was on the verge of his climax.

Sarah's own sexual desire was a burning need inside her and she moved her mouth on Jack faster, until he exclaimed in warning, "Sarah—"

Jack grasped her arm and she stopped and released him. He drew her roughly up beside him but she held him at bay and climbed astride his groin.

She settled herself on him, her cleft meeting his straining cock, her juices mingling with her saliva, which had already moistened him. She closed her eyes and ground herself against him, the delicious friction building in her stomach into an excruciating pleasure.

Jack cupped her breasts and she placed her hands over his and clenched them so that he squeezed.

Sarah's nipples were hard and she ached to have his lips on them, and as if he'd read her mind, he sat upright and kissed each in turn. She tossed her head back when he took one of the nubs into his mouth and nibbled the delicate skin there, his ministration stirring in her both pleasure and pain.

A wild shiver raced through her body and she clutched his shoulders and dug her nails into his skin.

Jack seemed to lose patience, and he clasped her hips and raised her. Sarah understood, and as she stared into his eyes, she grasped his hot length and guided him to her entrance.

She aligned herself with his cock, sat in a smooth motion and took him deep into her. She sat immobile, enjoying the sensation of having him inside while Jack skimmed her nipples with the fleshy pads of his thumbs.

She whimpered when he slowly pushed himself farther into her. Sarah's body jerked in response and her core enfolded him and enticed him in so he filled her completely.

For a few moments they were both still, then she bent forward and kissed his shoulder and neck before she moved on to his mouth. They met and entwined their tongues and she tasted him, hungrily pressing her kiss-sensitive lips to his.

Sarah rocked back and forth. She gripped his shoulders so she could glide up and down along his penis, pausing for heartbeats at a time then allowing him to arch up into her.

A slow burn began deep in her cleft and coursed through her belly in tight, gripping spasms. As their passion rose, Sarah began to utter little encouraging moans and Jack's strokes became more forceful and relentless.

Her whimpers grew louder, until suddenly she tensed and arched her spine. She clawed at Jack's shoulders as her orgasm rolled over her and she shivered. She couldn't think because of the pleasure coursing throughout her body.

Her own climax ebbed and flowed and Jack shouted out as he came hard, his cock throbbing and pumping as if there was an endless flow of his juice to expend.

Sarah slumped against him, murmuring little endearments. She nuzzled his sweating chest and neck and Jack put his arms around her and kissed her damp forehead.

When his breathing had returned to normal, he said softly, "Hey."

Sarah groaned and kissed his neck. "Oh, I am so...pooped," she responded, her voice muffled.

Jack laughed. "Pooped? You poor thing. I make love to you twice and you're tired?"

He kissed her neck and she shivered. She laughed quietly and he shook her in a teasing way. "Are you laughing at me, Lieutenant?"

Sarah raised her head to stare at him and, still smiling, she stroked his cheek with her fingertips

"I'd never laugh at you, Captain Chalmers. You're too damn sexy."

"Uh-huh. You're my kind of woman, Sarah Morgan."

Sarah placed a gentle kiss on his mouth, followed by a teasing lick. "I think I can handle that."

Jack's arms tightened around her and she snuggled into him once more.

They stayed entwined together for a few more moments before Sarah stirred, rose to her knees and stretched to ease the kinks from her muscles. There was a pleasant soreness between her legs and light perspiration coated her skin.

Jack gazed at her breasts with a lustful glint in his eyes.

She glanced at her watch. "Down, boy," she ordered. "It's zero three hundred hours. We won't be able to function later today so, as much as I hate to say it, I think we should get some sleep."

Sarah slid off him, drew back the sheet and covered herself with it.

Jack straightened the rumpled blankets and lay beside her. "Yes, ma'am," he said. "Come here."

Sarah lay beside him and pushed her body close to his. She was exhausted, both mentally and physically. The events of that night had far outweighed her expectations, and it felt as if everything that had happened was a dream. If it was, it was one she didn't want to ever wake up from.

Jack kissed her forehead tenderly and rested his head against hers.

Sarah was drifting off to sleep so she was never sure she heard exactly what he whispered to her.

It had sounded like "Goodnight, my love," and if those were the words he had used, she had won the battle for her man. When dawn broke, it would be a new beginning for them.

Chapter Fifteen

Sarah woke suddenly and for a moment was confused as to where she was and who the warm body pressed to her back belonged to. An arm lay heavily over her waist, a hand resting between her breasts.

Memories with explicit detail of what had happened at the ball the night before and the hours following exploded into her head.

It's Jack. It's not a dream.

Happiness and blissful contentment flooded through her and Sarah sighed. She snuggled her bottom into Jack's groin and was rewarded when his penis hardened against her.

"You're doing it again," Jack's voice said drowsily in her ear. "You've been teasing me all night. That's not conducive to a great sleep."

Sarah nestled herself even closer to him. "I have?" she asked and yawned. "Sorry. Can't help it. You're my drug and I'm addicted to you. I'm going to need my Jack Chalmers fix every so often."

Jack kissed her ear. "I'll settle for that. Morning…"

Sarah smiled at him. "Good morning. What time is it, anyway?"

"Ten hundred hours. We have to leave by noon, otherwise we'll be kicked out."

Sarah made a moue of reluctance. "Do we have to? I don't want to move."

Jack relaxed his hand and stroked her nipple gently. "Neither do I."

A familiar tingle traveled down into her belly and Sarah squirmed. "Please don't do that," she said breathlessly.

"No?" Jack said and trailed his fingers to her stomach and rested his palm there, making her muscles tense. "Why?"

"Yes, and because—" She squeaked, thrusting her hips to meet his fingers as they quested toward her cleft.

"Because what?"

"Because…I have to go to the bathroom and take a shower."

Jack laughed out loud. "You're such a liar, Sarah Morgan. Okay. I've shut my eyes, so go."

Sarah scrambled out of bed. She headed for the washroom, grabbing her sea bag on the way, and darted through the door, closing it behind her.

Once she'd used the toilet and flushed, she turned on the shower. She took her toiletries from her bag and placed them inside the enclosure, put on a plastic shower cap, tucked her tresses inside and stepped in to stand beneath the spray.

Jack more than likely also needed to use the facilities, so she had to be quick. She poured some liquid soap into her palm and rubbed it onto her body, relishing the sweet smell of strawberries and mango as it mixed with the water and bubbled into a frothy lather.

She touched her breasts, remembered the way Jack had caressed them, and she shivered. When she was washing her stomach, she pictured Jack using his tongue to lave her skin and she bit her bottom lip as the memory scorched her mind.

Calm down, honey. It's time to get out of here.

Sarah rinsed the soap off herself and stepped onto the tiled floor. She spun the controls to the off position and dried herself with a fluffy bath towel then pulled on fresh underwear, tight, faded jeans and a white T-shirt that left her tan midriff bare.

She brushed her teeth, pulled off the shower cap and shook her hair free before she brushed it with quick, hard strokes. She decided to leave it loose, thrust her feet into canvas boat shoes, applied some lip gloss and sprayed herself liberally with perfume. She threw everything haphazardly into the bag and exited the bathroom in a rush.

"Finished," she announced and posed provocatively against the jamb. "It's all yours." She paused when she saw what he was doing. "I see you're well trained."

Jack was up and dressed in shorts but was bare-chested. He stood beside a table which held the makings for coffee and tea and a kettle with steam curling from its spout, as if it had recently boiled. He had pulled back the heavy drapes and opened the balcony doors.

Sunlight streamed in and threw golden puddles onto the carpet. Sarah could hear waves crashing on the beach and smelled salt on the breeze that was blowing into the room.

At the sound of her voice, Jack grinned at her and gestured with an empty cup. There was a shyness about his demeanor that Sarah found endearing when he said, "I wasn't sure what your choice of drink is or what you wanted in it. With or without?"

Sarah giggled, the sound girlish and rich in the quiet room.

"After last night...and this morning, you don't even know how to make my drink?"

Jack's grin widened. "I didn't have time to ask. I was too...preoccupied."

Sarah blushed. "You're forgiven...under the circumstances."

She walked toward him, stood on tiptoe and kissed him full on the mouth. "I take coffee with."

Sarah cupped his chin before he could move and stared critically at his wound.

She winced at what she saw. "Ouch. You've got the beginnings of a neat black eye. It might not come to anything, but it's going to take some explaining."

"Nope, it'll be okay. I've got it all worked out. I'll be right back to make it for you."

As she'd predicted, he made a trip into the bathroom then hurried back to make her coffee. Once he'd finished, he gave her the mug, grabbed his own and took her hand in his.

"Shall we go outside? We need to talk."

Sarah's stomach plunged sickeningly.

Need to talk.

How many times had she heard that brief, brutal statement made in almost every single love story, on television or in books, when it came time to make excuses as to why a relationship or marriage had to end?

She wondered whether it was her moment to hear that their night together had been a big mistake and it was over before it had even started.

She let Jack lead her out onto the balcony, where there was a small table and chairs shielded by a rattan windbreak. It offered them privacy from the scrutiny of the *BIA*'s crew, if they were conscious and up and about. They both sat, Jack clasping his cup in both hands, Sarah turning to look out at the beach.

It was a beautiful day, with a golden sun shining in a cloudless blue sky, its rays sparkling on the swells of the ocean. Herring gulls screeched and hovered on the air currents, watching for food, and children laughed and played in the sand.

"Are you okay?" Jack asked.

Sarah turned to him. "I'm fine," she replied. "You wanted to talk to me?"

Here it comes.

Jack inhaled and looked down at the surface of the white wooden table, as if he could see something of interest there.

"Please don't feel like you have to say yes," he said and fell silent.

Sarah frowned, confused. "What might I need not to say yes to?"

Jack grinned. "I should have mentioned this to you earlier, but it slipped my mind during…everything. I'm going home to my family today. It's my eldest sister's wedding tomorrow. I'd told them I couldn't make it and they don't know I'm coming, so it should be one hell of a surprise. I'd like you to come with me."

Sarah stared at him. When she heard he still wanted to be with her, her initial fear evaporated, replaced with an immense relief. She was delighted he'd asked her and she slumped back in her chair, speechless at his invitation.

Jack noticed her silence, looked at her and frowned. "Is something wrong?"

"I thought *the talk* was going to be 'thank you, Sarah, for the one-night stand, but no thanks.' I was expecting to get my marching orders, not invited to your sister's wedding."

Jack's frown deepened. "Why would I say it was over? Shit, Sarah. After all that's happened, do you think I would treat you like you were some hooker?"

He took a sip of coffee, and glared at her with an expression of annoyance on his face.

Sarah touched his hand where it lay on the table. "I'm sorry," she said. "I made a mistake."

"Yeah, you sure did," Jack replied. "Please, *don't* do it again. When you get to know me, you'll learn that's not how I treat people — and certainly not you."

Chastened, Sarah nodded and changed the subject. "If your turning up for your sister's wedding will be a surprise, won't they freak out if I come with you?"

Jack's voice still had an undernote of irritation in it. "Mom has been on my case for years to bring *someone* home for family celebrations and Christmases and I've ignored her. She'll be smug and unbearable when she sees you."

"I'm honored I'll be the first then."

"You're the only woman I've ever wanted to bother bringing home." He took her hand in his. "You'll come with me, then? I know you've got some leave because I signed off on it, so there isn't any reason for you to say no..."

Sarah smiled. "I was going to visit my parents, but I can call them and cancel, so I'd love to. One thing, though. I'll need to buy a dress and shoes to wear. I wasn't expecting to go to a wedding and I've got nothing suitable with me."

Jack lips tightened in a grimace. "I don't do the shopping thing. I went with my mom once and said I liked something she tried on. She bought it and she's never forgiven me. Shopping with a female scares the crap out of me."

Sarah laughed. "Okay. I wouldn't want to frighten you to death. If we find a mall, I'll go and you can stay in the car."

"That might work. But I thought women took hours to shop."

"Not this one."

"Okay, I'll have to believe you. My lot live in South Mills, North Carolina. It's an hour's drive from here, just under fifty miles. On the way is the Landstown Commons shopping center, which should have what you want. It's about a twenty-five-minute drive."

Sarah gazed at him, wide-eyed. "Do you have a map in your head or something?"

"Nope. I've done the drive before," Jack said. "It looks like we have a plan. I'm going to my room for a quick shower and to pack my gear, then we can leave. I'll be about twenty minutes. We'll sneak out the side exit in case the crew have made it out of their beds."

He stood and touched her cheek with a finger. "I'm glad you're coming with me. I didn't want to let you go yet. But please don't ever second-guess me again."

Sarah turned her head and kissed his hand. "I won't. Go."

Jack leaned forward to place a warm kiss on her mouth "You got it. Don't go anywhere."

"I don't intend to."

Sarah stayed seated and watched him go into the room. He dressed, but before he could leave, she remembered something.

"Wait," she called out and hurried after him. "You'll need this to get back in here."

She found her purse, took out the key card and handed it to him. He tipped his chin, winked, then opened the door, went out and closed it behind him.

Sarah returned to the balcony and sat down to drink the rest of her coffee. She began to feel conspicuous and worried that even with the screen dividers, she might be too out in the open for anyone who knew her to see, so after a few moments, she went back inside.

She lifted her bag onto the bed and began to look for her panties. She eventually found them in a far corner of the room. She buried the wispy material in the depths of her sea bag then bent and picked up her ball gown, which lay crumpled on the floor.

Her lips twisted in a pained grimace when she saw the dirty marks on the skirt. The reason for the stains made her shudder and she hurriedly folded it, put it in with her underwear and threw her sandals on top. She then sat on the bed and stared out of the balcony doors at the blue sky.

Time seemed to stand still while Sarah waited for Jack's return. She wondered how she was going to stay away from him onboard the *BIA*, if twenty minutes seemed like a lifetime.

Feeling restless and lost without him, she went to the balcony doors and stared out to sea. She jumped when arms enfold her waist from behind and Jack kissed her neck.

Sarah shivered and leaned against him. "Hey," she said. "You weren't kidding about being quick, were you?"

Jack grinned and shook his head. "Nope. I never kid about being punctual."

Sarah turned to face him and studied him as any woman would with a man who she desired like hell.

His hair was damp from his shower and he was clean-shaven. She let her eyes roam his body and noticed he wore faded jeans, a white T-shirt, a distressed brown leather bomber jacket and tan work boots. She could smell his cologne and she moistened her lips at the sight of him.

As if reading her thoughts, Jack's grin widened and he tipped his chin at her. "Don't stare at me like that. Shall we go, or is there something else you'd like to do first?"

Sarah frowned at him in mock annoyance and walked past him. "Don't be so full of yourself, Jack Chalmers."

She left the key card where Jack had placed it upon his return, next to the coffee and tea supplies, found her purse, opened it and took out her oversized sunglasses.

Jack laughed out loud. "Can you see through those things?"

"Disguise purposes only," Sarah replied and wrinkled her nose at him.

"I guess that might work."

Sarah ignored him and collected her sea bag from the bed. Jack gestured for her to precede him and she sauntered past and headed for the door.

She'd only gone a few feet when Jack slapped her bottom, pulled her bag from her hand, dropped it on the floor and grasped her arm firmly.

"C'mere a minute," he ordered and pulled her to him.

He removed her sunglasses, cupped her chin in his hand and kissed her thoroughly until she was breathless.

He finally let her go and said, "I couldn't resist your butt. Are you sure you don't want to stay here a bit longer?"

"Yes. No. Yes, I do, but it's nearly noon. And you weren't kissing my backside," Sarah answered, her heart beating frantically from the intensity of the kiss.

"Yeah, well. Your *behind* wasn't available. Okay, ma'am, your wish is my command. Lead the way."

Jack gave her back her eyewear, picked up his bag and uniform carrier and waited for Sarah to grab her purse and bag before she marched across the room on unsteady legs.

Before she opened the door, Sarah turned to him. "We'll go out the back way," she said. "I guess we shouldn't be seen together."

The amused expression on Jack's face vanished and he tensed his jaw. "I guess not," he said at last. "Are you sure you want to deal with this?"

Sarah frowned. "Don't go there, Jack. It is what it is. I wouldn't have it any other way."

Jack nodded, moved closer and kissed her. "Let's bug out then."

Sarah was thoroughly bemused and it wasn't until they left the room and were hurrying along the hallway that she could think straight once more.

She summoned the elevator and, while they waited, she stood as close to him as she could, brushing her bare arm against his leather jacket.

The elevator car arrived and Sarah and Jack stepped inside. She pressed the button for the ground floor.

As the doors slid shut, Jack moved in on her. She put a hand on his chest to ward him off and said, "I can't think straight when you're near me, Jack. Behave yourself."

Jack grinned and turned away.

Chapter Sixteen

Once the elevator had settled on the ground floor, its doors opened and Jack and Sarah went to the small door they had used the previous night and let themselves out.

They turned left, and with Jack taking the lead, they kept close to the side of the building and headed toward the parking lot at the front of the hotel.

Sarah had no idea where Jack had parked his vehicle, so she followed behind him. She intended to leave her own vehicle, which wasn't ideal because there was always a chance someone would become suspicious at the length of its stay and report it to the police. They would then track her down, which might prove to be a considerable problem for all involved.

They walked the perimeter until Jack pointed an electronic key at a group of cars parked near the entrance. There was a beep and a low-slung sports car's headlights flashed intermittently.

They approached the fire-red vehicle and Sarah studied its sleek lines and built-for-speed body work. She glanced at Jack and raised her eyebrows.

"Very fancy," she said.

"It's a Ford Mustang GT," Jack explained, and went to the trunk and opened it.

Sarah joined him. "I wouldn't have thought fast cars were your…thing."

Jack threw his bag in the boot and rested his uniform on top before taking Sarah's from her. "They're not. But I like Fords and this one is okay, so I bought it. It'll be my one and only buy, though."

"One of your pride and joys?"

Jack shut the lid. "One of 'em? What the hell are the others?"

Sarah blushed a little. "Well, the BIA is your first love, I take it, so the Ford must be a close second."

Jack stared at her for a minute, looked away and shook his head. "They were."

Without saying another word, he left her where she stood and went to the passenger door. He opened it and glanced over his shoulder at her. "Coming?"

Sarah nodded and climbed into the leather bucket seat. She fastened her seatbelt while Jack went to the driver's side and got in.

Before he started the engine, he delved into the pocket beside him, found what he was searching for and put on a pair of silver-toned aviator sunglasses.

"Ready?" he asked and turned the key in the ignition.

The powerful engine roared into life then settled to a subdued rumble, and Jack put it into gear and drove out of the parking space.

As he guided the vehicle toward the exit, Sarah glanced at his hands on the leather steering wheel and her cheeks flushed with heat.

Those hands have touched me.

She focused her gaze on the changing scenery through the windscreen, determined not to think any further lustful thoughts about him. If she didn't stop, they would drive her mad.

They pulled out into traffic and Sarah studied her surroundings. Jack had told her they would get to the mall via the General Booth Boulevard, and now she eagerly looked around her.

The traffic was heavy and the sidewalks crowded with people enjoying shopping, eating in restaurants and entering the amusement areas with excited children. The cobalt-blue sea glittered in the distance and a gentle breeze blew in through the open car windows.

Sunshine bathed everything in a golden glow and the temperature was as high as the warmth inside her. Sarah was happy, the last twenty-four hours with Jack having culminated in contentment and a sexually-satiated euphoria.

Jack drove with skill but was quiet as he negotiated the start-and-stop traffic. Sarah stayed silent, relaxed in the contoured seat and closed her eyes.

Her thoughts turned once more to her and Jack, and for the first time she felt worried for their fragile relationship.

She had an idea that they were both deliberately ignoring what might happen if they got caught and how they would deal with the situation when they got back to the ship. If she were honest with herself, it felt as if she'd been existing in a protective bubble since they'd met, with concerns regarding their futures kept at bay.

She had no doubt that when it eventually burst and they had to return to their jobs, they would have to make some difficult choices concerning where their lives were headed, be it together or apart.

The thought that it might not work out between them was more painful then she cared to admit. She didn't want to lose him.

Sarah sighed. He'd already stolen a part of her, and if he left, it would devastate her. Yes, she could move on, but her life would never be the same.

"Hey," Jack said, startling her. "Is everything okay? You looked sad there for a minute."

Sarah turned to him and smiled. "I'm fine," she said.

It was disconcerting not to be able to see his eyes behind his glasses, so she couldn't tell whether he believed her or not, but he made no comment and turned his attention back to the road.

Approximately ten minutes later, he put on a turn indicator and pulled into a parking lot with a large shopping mall in front of them.

He drove into a space close to the building and turned off the engine. It ticked as it cooled and he unlocked his seatbelt and faced her.

"Go do your thing," he said. "I'll wait here."

Sarah leaned over and touched his face. "Thank you," she said. "I won't be long."

Jack grinned at her. "Uh-huh. Yeah, right."

Sarah huffed, took off her sunglasses and dropped them in her purse at her feet. She withdrew her pocketbook, opened her door and got out. She went to the driver's side and rested her arms on the window, leaning in.

She smiled sweetly. "I must have worn you out, Jack. You look so tired. Why don't you catch a nap and get your strength back?"

"Funny," Jack replied, the corner of his mouth lifting in a smile. "Get going, lady."

"By the way, what color are the bridesmaid's dresses?"

Jack removed his sunglasses, stared at her and looked nonplussed. "Huh?"

Sarah rolled her eyes at him. "I don't want to clash with the attendants."

"How the hell would I know? It's a wedding thing."

"Okay, if I get it wrong, I'll blame it on your lack of knowledge concerning your own sister's color theme—"

Jack was silent for a moment. "It's blue or...yellow. She's marrying a submariner so—"

"Oh, yes, Stupid me. It's Navy, so it's gotta be blue...or yellow...or even pink."

Sarah leaned farther into the car and stroked his cheek with her finger. "See ya," she sang out and turned away.

She sashayed her hips for a few steps, because she guessed Jack might well be watching her, laughed to herself and walked at a brisk pace toward the mall.

Sarah entered the air-conditioned interior, avoided a screeching child as it ran toward her and, business-like, found a map of the complex at an information assistance booth.

She studied it, her finger tracing the route she needed that would take her to a department store, looked around to verify where she was in relation to the exit. With her track memorized, she set out.

She strode to an escalator, took it to the first level and, deftly avoiding the crowds, hurried toward her destination.

A few minutes after entering the store, she found the dress she wanted, followed a few moments later by shoes and a bag of almost the same color. She went to the lingerie section, purchased what she needed there, grabbed a few other items she thought she might require, paid then exited the store at a fast trot.

Minutes later, she'd returned to the car. She tapped on the door to alert Jack, who had apparently taken her at her word and fallen asleep.

He woke instantly, noticed her staring in at him and said sarcastically, "Wow. That's gotta be some record for a woman to choose a dress."

He got out, went to the trunk to open it and stared at the packages she carried. "Did you buy the whole store?" he asked.

Sarah laid the dress on top of the carrier that held his uniform and stashed her shopping carefully around everything else.

"Ha-ha," she said, her tone equally sarcastic and left him grinning as he slammed the lid. Her hand was on the handle of the passenger door when he leaned around her and opened it.

His lips grazed her cheek and she heard him inhale. "You smell so…goddamn sexy," he whispered.

Sarah shivered. "Jack," she warned, but loved his closeness and the fact that he couldn't stay away from her.

"Okay. Okay. I quit."

Sarah got into the car and strapped herself in.

Jack got in beside her and, with the lopsided smile still on his face, started the engine and drove them out of the parking lot.

Chapter Seventeen

Jack drove back on to the General Booth Boulevard. They remained in traffic for a short period of time before he made a turn east onto Interstate 264, which began at the Raleigh Beltline.

Once they were on the freeway, Sarah investigated the complicated dials and buttons on the Ford's dashboard in a search for the radio. She finally found it and studied what looked to resemble computer-speak before she reached out to press a small knob marked *On*.

Her finger was less than an inch away from the button when Jack shouted, "Bang," and she squealed and jerked it away.

She glared at him and saw he'd raised his sunglasses to the top of his head. He was staring at her with a boyish shit-eating grin on his face.

She burst into giggles and lightly slapped his arm. "Not funny," she said and her voice shook with amusement. "I could have pressed something dangerous and we might have gone into orbit in this thing."

Jack winked, lowered his eyewear back into place and turned his gaze back to the road.

Sarah still smiled as she went for the radio once more, and this time Jack stayed quiet when she switched it on. Music instantly filled the car, and as it was a tune she liked, she left it on that station and settled in.

She rocked her body, her bottom shimmying and her upper torso moving to the loud beat. She had no idea she was being watched until Jack said, "I like your moves, lady."

When she looked at him, he had lifted his shades once more and was gazing at her with a warm expression on his face. He saw he had her attention, raised an eyebrow and grinned.

Sarah blushed. "You're one badass, Jack Chalmers," she said. "Eyes back on the road or you'll get us killed."

"Yes, ma'am," Jack said, lowered his glasses into place and faced forward.

The freeway ran through a long, wooded stretch until it curved south of Wilson before it met Interstate 95 and downgraded to an expressway. It looped north around Greenville and they continued east on Pactolus Highway, then took the slipway onto Interstate 17.

I-17 began as a two-lane road then converted to a four-lane freeway, and traffic became heavier and more congested. Sarah let Jack drive in peace and closed her eyes, opening them now and again to check on the scenery and what direction they were traveling in.

The freeway eventually changed to a scenic rural road which crossed over the Editro River and regained a four-lane configuration. The road passed through several rural communities, and Sarah straightened and placed her hand on Jack's leg.

He flinched at her touch and she smiled. "How're we doing?" she asked.

"I'm doing fine," Jack replied. "How are *you* doing?"

Sarah prodded his thigh muscle with her fingertips. "I meant how far have we left to go?"

"Not long."

Sarah glanced at his leg and glided her fingers to his groin. "Feeling even better now?"

"Uh-huh."

His thigh muscle tensed beneath his jeans and she slowly circled her fingers between his legs. He bucked his hips and shifted his bottom, as if he were uncomfortable.

She trailed her fingers to his crotch, where she stroked his balls then squeezed his cock, which had grown hard at her ministrations.

"Shit, Sarah," he exclaimed as he involuntarily pushed his groin toward her hand. The car veered slightly to the right before he brought it back on course. "I'm driving."

"Then don't drive," Sarah said, her voice husky.

Without another word, Jack flipped on the right-turn indicator and spun the steering wheel so sharply that the tires screeched. He drove along a narrow dirt track bordered by thick pines until, after a few minutes, he stopped the car and turned off the engine. He unbuckled his seatbelt, did the same for Sarah and pulled her toward him.

He put his arm around her shoulders and murmured, "Tease," then kissed her deep and rough, thrusting his tongue between her eager lips and lashing the inside of her mouth, as if he were hungry for her.

Sarah's nipples hardened and chaffed at the lace cups of her bra. The friction created a heady sensation of fullness and sensitivity, and while she loved Jack's demanding kisses, she wished he would caress her breasts, play with, bite and suck them in his usual single-minded manner.

Her nipples were a direct line to her core, which was swollen and aching, and she kneaded his crotch with her fingers, parting her thighs when his hand caressed her leg.

He massaged her sensitive inner thigh before he touched her covered clit. She moaned out loud when a sensation like an electric shock torched her and settled as a sizzling blaze in her stomach.

Sarah pressed her hand harder to Jack's rigid cock and rubbed him slowly. Her palm created a fiery friction, and he groaned and thrust his hips in time with her actions.

His breathing was fast and uneven and she strained her body to get close to him. She wrenched her mouth from his and gasped. "Make love to me, Jack."

"Here?" Jack asked, his voice slurred.

"Here… *Now.*"

Jack pressed his fingers to the damp denim between her legs and she pushed herself onto them.

"We can't, Sarah. Someone could pull in any minute."

Sarah stopped moving her hand and tried to control her breathing. "You're right."

Jack kissed her, removed his hand and touched her cheek. "I want to make love to you. *Now,*" he said slowly and deliberately. "Believe me."

Sarah swallowed and tried to ignore the ache of unfulfillment that lingered in the lower regions of her belly. "I know."

"We'll sort this out later. I promise."

Chapter Eighteen

Approximately twenty minutes later, Jack flipped on the right-hand indicator and turned the car from the I-17 blacktop onto a dusty dirt road. Sarah stared at her surroundings with interest.

Bright green grass stippled with tiny, white, artificial-looking flowers stretched like a carpet on either side for the first fifty feet or so before dense forest loomed like the hoary walls of a fortress and prevented the living blanket from encroaching any farther.

The roadway disappeared beneath an over-arching vault formed by huge arthritic boughs, gnarled with age, which, as the years had gone by, had grown and entwined to form a canopy of tannin brown, umber and muted green and silver.

Jack steered the vehicle skillfully into the shady avenue and Sarah saw immensely tall Longleaf, Loblolly and Virginia pine interspersed with butternut hickory, live oak and American elm that formed impenetrable barriers on each side of the road for as far as she could see.

Darkness lurked among the lichen-covered trunks, and shadows coalesced and shifted in the sun's rays that filtered through gaps between the knotted branches to form pools of antique gold on the piles of leaves and vegetation that made up the undergrowth.

Sarah smiled in delight as sunlight splashed through the leaves to form dancing patterns on the road ahead. She breathed in a woody odor of pine and resin as it drifted through the open window and heard bird song coming from the trees around her.

"Are we going off route?" she asked, speaking in a low voice.

It was ridiculous, but she felt if she spoke out loud it would disturb the primeval silence and destroy the giant trees' solitude.

Jack glanced sideways at her and smiled. "Nope. We call this a driveway in my neck of the woods. No pun intended."

"A driveway?" She paused. "It's very long. Is it yours?"

Jack's grin widened. "Not mine. It belongs to my parents. Don't you have one?"

Sarah shook her head, a little awed. "I don't personally. My mom and dad do but it's not as grand as this one. Those trees are stunning. Is there a large house to go with this big driveway?"

"It's okay for the five of us. Hey… You're not nervous, are you?"

Sarah shrugged and tried not to feel uneasy, as though she was going to be dropped from a great height into a lifestyle she'd never dreamed of.

"No, but you didn't tell me your family were landowners and kick-ass rich to boot."

Jack laughed out loud. "Kick-ass rich? Not even close. We're just normal people. My mom might be a bit nuts, but we live like everyone else. They'll love you like I —"

Jack stopped speaking and fell silent, and Sarah wondered what he'd been going to say. She thought better of asking and turned her thoughts instead to what type of house might be waiting at the end of the dirt road and what it might look like. The vast amount of land she could see was justification enough for the nerves to create a fresh storm in her stomach.

She cleared her throat. "Are you sure your mom won't mind me appearing unannounced?" she asked. "It's not exactly common courtesy for a stranger to turn up at a wedding."

"Like I told you, my mom has *demanded* I invite someone every time we have some sort of party or a get-together. She'll be even more unmanageable when she sees you. Stop worrying, Sarah. Everything'll be okay."

Unconvinced, Sarah became quiet and pensive and stared ahead through the windscreen.

Moments later, the answer to her question about the house presented itself when their vehicle burst from the tree-shrouded road and its green glow into glaring sunlight and she saw the building in all its glory.

Her eyes widened. "Oh, shit!" she exclaimed.

"Is that a shit, you hate it or a shit, you love it?" Jack asked, amusement evident in his voice.

"That's an 'oh, hell I'm screwed' type of shit," Sarah replied.

In front of her, with a front yard of approximately an acre, was an enormous gray-and-white three-story cedar house with a gray shingle roof. A wrap-around veranda edged with a rattan wood rail stretched along the front and curved along the sides with a roof the same color as the main one. The fancy woodwork was separated by steps that led to a white front door.

Sarah's gaze took in the mullioned windows on the first and second floors, each with gray shutters, with four smaller pitched-roof ones in what would likely be the loft. At either end of the central building were single story structures, similar in design.

The forest encircled the house and continued to the rear, giving it seclusion and privacy without making it isolated.

"Oh," Sarah murmured, "it's gorgeous."

Jack drove across the black asphalt parking area and stopped between two cars. He turned off the engine, undid his seatbelt and faced Sarah.

"You like?" he asked and took her hand in his. He raised it to his heart, and his thumb brushed her palm and ignited heat trails in its wake.

Sarah tried to ignore how his touch made her feel and failed dismally. "I like," she answered, breathless. "It looks…like it's part of the forest."

"You okay?"

"Yes. I'm fine."

She glanced at their entwined fingers and squeezed his. "Thank you for inviting me here."

Jack brought her hand to his mouth and kissed each knuckle in turn. She jumped as if she'd been burned.

"I wouldn't have come without you," he said and stared at her with eyes that were now a dark blue.

Silence, heavy with meaning, stretched between them and Sarah squirmed, her panties dampening as his gaze locked with hers. She was pinned to her seat by the emotion showing on his face.

"How do I introduce myself?" she asked at last, breaking the connection.

"Hello? Hi?" Jack answered.

"Ha-ha. I know that. I mean, what am I? Your lover, girl friend or second cousin?"

Jack was silent for a minute. "My woman. Would that be okay?"

Sarah's heart missed a beat. "That sounds a bit chauvinistic and like a bit too much information, don't you think?"

"Yeah, maybe. What about…significant other?"

Sarah laughed. "Sounds good. Not too formal."

Jack grinned at her, still languidly stroking her skin with his thumb, his palm warm and comforting.

At last, he seemed to shake himself and released her. "Come on. Let's get moving. I'm sure someone will have seen us arrive and we'll be crushed in the stampede if we don't get inside first."

He opened his door and got out. A few seconds later, Sarah followed suit, and while he went to the trunk to remove their luggage, she continued to stare at the house.

Jack joined her, carrying both sea bags, his uniform and her dress, along with her other parcels. Hands full, he nudged her with his elbow. "Ready?" he asked.

"Nope," Sarah answered. "But hey, nobody said it was going to be easy."

A loud, excited squeal interrupted them, followed by feet pattering on wood. Sarah turned to see a woman run down the steps leading from the veranda.

"Jack! You made it."

Sarah watched as a pretty, blonde-haired female dressed in a knee-length pale blue silk robe and wearing satin ballet slippers, a thick white substance coating her face, ran toward Jack.

As she drew near, Jack dropped the bags and laid the carriers on the hood of his car. "Don't you come near me with that stuff on your face, Ashleigh. It might be contagious," he said.

Ashleigh Chalmers smiled with delight and threw herself into Jack's arms. "Screw you, big brother," she said.

Jack laughed out loud and lifted his sister into the air, noticeably avoiding kissing her cheek with its slimy mask, before he deposited her feet back on the ground.

"What is that stuff? It stinks," he asked.

"A yogurt face mask," Ashleigh replied. "Why didn't you tell us you were coming?"

"I wanted to surprise you. I thought yogurt was something you ate. That's disgusting."

Ashleigh slapped her brother's arm then wrinkled her nose at him. "Yeah, well, Jack, you don't know a thing about beauty regimes and you could do with learning a few tips yourself."

Another scream—louder this time—sounded from inside the house. A second female, younger than the first, with a darker blonde mane and clad in faded torn shorts and a loose white T-shirt, came darting out of the front door. It had been left ajar and she shoved it open so wide that it slammed into an ornate plant pot that was filled with cascades of blooms. The girl bolted toward the group.

"Jack! Jack! You're here."

Jack's younger sister tore down the steps, ran the short distance between them, launched herself into his arms and hugged him tightly.

Sarah smiled at the exuberant greetings and excitement from Jack's family. She had noticed a dramatic change in her inscrutable commanding officer now that he was home. It warmed her to see how relaxed and less unapproachable he had become, even though she now had first-hand knowledge of how he was when he dropped his guard.

More footsteps sounded and she turned again to look toward the veranda. A man and a woman in their early sixties appeared, the woman with handsome features and short salt-and-pepper hair jumping up and down delightedly, the man more dignified but with a wide smile on his craggy-featured, tan face.

A large sand-colored retriever followed them both, responding to the noise with excited barks and joyful yips.

The older couple walked at a slower pace as they descended the steps, but as soon as they stepped onto the level surface of the parking lot, the woman shouted, "Why couldn't you have slammed the door open a bit harder, Hayley? Maybe broken the flowerpot as well."

She began to jog toward Jack, a wide smile on her face. "Jack. My baby boy."

Sarah barely stopped herself from snorting with amusement.

Baby boy?

Jack broke free from his second sister and stepped forward a pace to meet his mother, who was making a beeline for him like a runaway juggernaut.

"Holy shit, Mom. I thought we'd laid the name calling to rest."

As he spoke, the dog reached him first, jumped at him and placed its forepaws on his chest, its tail wagging in circles like a propeller.

Jack staggered backward and fell against the car, moving his head to avoid the wet tongue that finally succeeded in slathering his face with dog kisses.

"I see Miss Fortune is still living up to her name," he said and managed to free himself from the animal's embrace.

Jack's mother halted in front of her son, dealt him a hearty slap on his stomach and snorted. "You'll always be my baby boy. Don't be facetious and don't swear."

She threw her arms around him so ferociously that Jack pulled a face and staggered once more.

She said in a low voice but loud enough for Sarah to hear, "It's good to have you home safe, Jack."

"Yes, welcome home, son," Jack's dad said as he joined the laughing group and slapped Jack on the shoulder. "Glad you could make it."

With the excited people calming down and Sarah feeling like a fifth wheel, she suddenly found herself the focus of Ashleigh's attention.

The sister stared at her with the same piercing blue eyes as her brother's and asked, "Who's this, Jack?"

At her question, everyone fell silent and turned to look at her. Sarah's cheeks grew hot with embarrassment at being the focus of everyone's attention.

Before either she or Jack could introduce her, his mother clasped her son's chin and asked, "Have you been fighting, son?"

Jack pulled away from his mother's grip and surreptitiously winked at Sarah. He held out his hand to her and said, "I got it in the line of duty rescuing a damsel in distress. Mom, Dad, Ashleigh, Hayley... I'd like you to meet Lieutenant Sarah Morgan, my...significant other."

Sarah made a face at him and stepped forward, sliding her palm into his. He guided her in among his family, put his arm about her shoulders and pulled her close to him.

Four pairs of eyes regarded her intently and Sarah was glad of Jack's embrace. She managed a smile and said, "I'm happy to meet you all."

His mother glanced at the sky then smiled. "Lord, thank you. At *last*. It's lovely to meet you, Sarah. Call me Wendy," she said.

"A bit over the top, Mom," Jack announced.

Wendy walked toward Sarah and, as she passed Jack, unerringly dealt him another back-handed tap on his abdomen before she enveloped Sarah in a warm, motherly hug.

The older woman drew away and cupped Sarah's chin in a work-worn palm. "You're extremely pretty, honey. I can see why my son calls you his *significant other*."

Wendy looked at Jack and poked out her tongue.

"Oh, so that's what it's known as now-a-days. I'm Stewart," Jack's dad commented, a knowing expression on his face.

Ashleigh approached Sarah and put a friendly hand on her arm. She smiled then said, "Any significant other of my brother's is very welcome here."

"Thank you," Sarah answered, thoroughly overwhelmed by the greeting she had received.

"Okay, you lot. Let's get inside. What will the neighbors think about this shit storm? They'll create holy hell," Wendy said.

"You're swearing, Mom," Jack said.

Wendy glanced at him and frowned. "I'm your Mom. I'm entitled." She faced them both and continued, "Come on. We'll have something to eat. Sarah, I'll show you afterward where you'll sleep."

Ashleigh slipped her arm through Sarah's and led her toward the house. Wendy and Hayley each had their own linked through Jack's, and Stewart brought up the rear, carrying their bags and carriers and trying not to fall over the dog as she cannoned into him and got under his feet.

Chapter Nineteen

Sarah went through the highly varnished front door and found herself in a large black-and-white tiled entrance hall with a huge chandelier suspended from a lofty ceiling, its crystal drops sparkling in the sunlight.

The lower half of the walls was paneled in pale oak, the rest papered in what looked to be a floral embossed silk covering. Framed pictures showed horses, dogs and Jack's parents and sisters, hanging as if positioned in an art gallery.

Vases stood on every available surface—the floor, two small tables and a carved wooden shelf beneath an ornate mirror—all filled with colorful flowers, their scent hanging heavy on the warm air.

Sarah looked at Jack and noticed that he was eyeing her, a strange expression on his face. She smiled at him and he responded with a wink then grinned at her before he turned to speak to his father.

She sensed the cozy, lived-in atmosphere in the house, despite its opulence and elegance, and she continued to scan her environment until Wendy changed into a nightmarish version of an army sergeant major and started to order her family around.

"Ashleigh? Why don't you take Sarah and make her comfortable? Jack, you go with her and you'll be out of my hair. Stu, leave their bags in the hall and we'll sort them out after we've eaten. Hayley, honey, help me get supper ready."

"Yes, ma'am," Jack and Stewart said simultaneously and looked at each other, their mouths working as if they were trying to keep straight faces.

"Mom is on a roll," Ashleigh said in Sarah's ear as she led her toward another door. "She's been fantastic with the wedding arrangements, but when she's off and running, she's a tyrant. Woe betide anyone who crosses her and gets in her way. Jack knows to his cost. We love her to pieces, but—"

Sarah laughed. "She sounds exactly like my mom. You're not alone."

Jack's heavy footsteps followed behind them into an enormous living and dining room. Once inside, Ashleigh said, "I'd better get this muck off my face, otherwise my brother won't shut up about what I look like. I'll see you when we eat."

She smiled at Jack and Sarah and left. As soon as she'd gone, Jack walked to Sarah's side.

"Well?" he asked, his voice quiet.

"Your family's lovely, Jack. They're so friendly and funny."

"They've taken to you, especially Mom. If she hadn't, you would have gotten the cold shoulder and she wouldn't have hugged you. You're a hit."

Sarah touched his chest with her fingers before she cupped his face between her palms. "Am I a hit you with you, Jack?"

"What do you think?"

"I hope so," she murmured and kissed his chin.

"Without a doubt," he said, and his mouth met hers and he parted her lips with his tongue.

Sarah pushed her hips into his and wondered how she was going keep herself from touching him over the next few days.

Jack trailed his fingers to her bottom and pulled her into him so she was pinned to his hardness.

"Can you feel me?" he asked in her ear.

Sarah pressed her hand to the front of his pants and stroked his erection. "Can you feel this?" she whispered and squeezed his cock.

He moaned. "Fuck, yeah," he answered and rocked his hips so that his penis slipped through her grip.

Stewart's voice echoed from the hall and Jack and Sarah sprang apart, Jack turning his body away from the doorway to hide his aroused state.

Sarah rubbed his back gently. "I'm going to go help your mom," she said.

"Good luck with that," Jack replied. "The kitchen is her domain and she guards it like you would the Crown Jewels...with a rolling pin."

Sarah laughed and edged past Jack's father.

"Don't talk like that about your mother, boy...even if it's true," Stewart said.

Sarah heard Jack laugh out loud before she followed the sounds made by his mother and sister. She stepped into an enormous kitchen decorated in cream and ochre, with pale oak cabinets and sand-colored marble work surfaces. A wonderful aroma of homemade bread, brownies and cookies filled the air and she inhaled the scent appreciatively.

Wendy looked up from where she was tossing salad in a bowl on a breakfast bar in the center of the room and smiled at her.

"Can I help at all?" Sarah asked.

"Absolutely not," Wendy answered. "When you're a guest in my house, you don't help out."

"Told you," Jack said from behind Sarah and rested a hand on her lower back.

"Oh, hell," Hayley exclaimed. "Here he is. You're following Sarah around like a puppy dog, Jack. Give the poor girl some space, why don't you?"

"Language, Hayley. Yes, baby boy. Go and sit in the living room. You're cluttering up the place. You too, Sarah. Relax and unwind. We'll eat in thirty minutes."

Jack turned on his heel and marched out of the kitchen. Sarah followed him.

* * * *

Sarah was happy and content, and surveyed her surroundings with interest as she sat between Jack's legs and rested against his chair. Beneath her was a plush chocolate-and-cream-colored rug. The décor of the room was ivory and beige, with dark brown sofas and chairs strewn with squishy pillows. There was pale oak furniture, which seemed to be the predominant wood so far in the house. French doors had been opened and an evening breeze wafted in, bringing with it the scent of pine and flowers and a woody essence.

Everyone had finished eating and a huge coffee table in the center of the carpet was littered with half-empty plates of sandwiches and dips, along with a few brownies and homemade cookies. The men now drank beer straight from bottles and the women—including Sarah—sipped wine from long-stemmed crystal glasses.

The conversation flowed around her, and as it concerned the wedding, she didn't participate but listened eagerly to last-minute details being gone over and Stewart's teasing in response.

Sarah caressed Jack's right calf muscle as she listened and sensually rubbed his skin, her hand safely concealed by her body and his left leg.

She could tell he was focused on what she was doing, because he too was quiet. On occasion, he shifted in his chair and the muscles in his thigh tightened and pressed against her arm.

His skin was warm to the touch and she trailed her fingers up his leg to the sensitive area behind his knee. A muscle jumped and he squeezed her upper torso with both his thighs in response.

Stewart roared with laughter and the three women squealed and giggled. Jack took the opportunity to lean forward and, under cover of the noise, said in her ear, "Will you stop doing that?"

Sarah turned to him and saw his gaze was smoldering as he stared at her. "Why would I want to do *that*?" she asked.

Jack kept eye contact with her and replied quietly, "You damn well know why. You're a tease and it's going to be extremely embarrassing if I have to move from this chair."

Sarah squeezed his calf muscle before she glided her fingernails firmly down to his ankle. "Am I?" she asked, and lowered her gaze and stared at his mouth, which had lost its smile. She watched as his jaw clenched and his nostrils flared.

"You know you are," Jack whispered. "You'll pay for it later."

Sarah bit her bottom lip and smiled sensuously. "I hope so," she said, equally quiet.

Jack settled back in his chair. "Count on it."

He pulled a cushion from behind him and placed it on his lap then rested his bottle on top of it.

"Sarah?"

Ashleigh called her name and Sarah turned her attention from Jack to focus on his sister.

"How long have you been on the *BIA*?"

"Umm, six and a half months. It's my first tour at sea," Sarah said.

"How many months have you and Jack been dating?" Hayley asked, her voice casual while nonchalantly studied the cell phone she held in her hands.

"Hayley," Jack warned, "that's none of your business."

"Six and a half months," Sarah replied before she could stop herself, hoping the lie was not evident.

There was silence at her answer and Jack's knee connected with her ribs. Seconds later, the Chalmers family burst out laughing.

Stewart almost choked and coughed to clear his throat. "Well, hell, son. That was fast work."

Ashleigh giggled. "Atta boy, big brother. You didn't hang around, did you?"

Jack's tone was halfway amused and halfway irritated when he interrupted the wisecracks. "Okay, that's enough, you lot. You'll give Sarah the wrong idea about me."

Wendy intervened firmly, "Yes, be quiet. You're embarrassing Sarah."

"Okay. Time for bed. We've got an early start tomorrow, which means *all of you*. No exceptions. I'll do the clearing up."

"Yes, Mom," said Hayley, still focused on her cell phone.

"Sure thing, Mom," Ashleigh replied and twirled a strand of hair with her fingers.

"Yeah, Mom," Jack murmured obediently, which prompted Sarah to stare at him in disbelief because he had acquiesced so easily.

"Certainly, honey," Stewart said.

Wendy glared at each of them in turn, as if to check their expressions to see if they were making fun of her. Once she was satisfied everyone was serious, she looked at Sarah.

"Sarah, honey, we'll put you in the guest house. It's at the bottom of the yard and Jack can show you where it is. The bedrooms in here will be filled tomorrow, now that he's home. It's good to have you here, and I'm sorry everything is a mess. We'll get to know each other better once the wedding is over."

There was nothing other than friendliness in the older woman's tone and Sarah smiled in appreciation.

"Okay. Let's move like we've got a purpose."

Sarah used Jack's knee as leverage, got to her feet and held out her hand to pull him up. Once he stood beside her, his eyes roamed her face, and he touched her cheek with his finger and outlined her mouth with its tip before he rested it on her lips and said, "I'll get your gear and take you down."

Sarah watched him as he walked away and left the room. She started to follow him but noticed Wendy staring at her with a knowing expression and she blushed. Her feelings for Jack must have been written plainly on her face for all to see.

Everyone left the room carrying plates and bowls and, feeling awkward, Sarah went out into the hall, where Jack had picked up her bags and dress and was waiting for her.

She called goodnight to the family before he gestured for her to follow him. They went back into the living room and he preceded her through the French doors onto the veranda.

They descended stone steps into the grassy backyard, which stretched approximately another acre and was bordered on all sides by shadowy trees that stood inky black against the encroaching night.

A huge marquee, erected for the wedding, gleamed halfway down the garden and tiny white lights, entwined among the branches of trees on the yard's perimeter and decorating the eves of the tent, twinkled and flashed in the darkness.

Jack took Sarah's hand and led her toward a small wooden building at the tree line at the end of the yard. A faint amber glow shone through glass onto the grass outside.

He was quiet as they walked and Sarah wondered if there was something bothering him. She drew close to him and nudged him with her elbow. "Are you okay?"

Jack looked at her and he smiled. "Everything's great," he replied. "Why'd you ask?"

"You seem quieter than usual."

Jack tightened his grip on her hand. "I'm going to be pretty lonely tonight, and it's going to be hell knowing you're so close and I can't be with you."

His words tugged at her heartstrings. "So, why don't you come and see me later?"

"Yeah, I might just do that."

They stopped outside the guest house and Jack placed her bags on the ground with her dress on top. He pulled her into his arms and kissed her mouth.

"Think about me?" he asked.

"Definitely," Sarah murmured and kissed him back.

He pulled her closer, his lips warm and his mouth growing hard on hers. When he finally broke free, he groaned. "You've got me so turned on that it's insane."

Sarah's own voice was unsteady when she replied, "Come back to me later, Jack. I'll wait up for you and we'll do...something about that."

Jack captured her lips once more and kissed her harder. His breathing was rapid when he drew back from her. "I'd better go. I bet all the windows in the house facing us are occupied by nosy members of my family. See you later," he said and walked away from her.

Sarah watched him go. Her lower belly ached with desire and there was a burning need between her legs that only Jack could relieve.

When he disappeared into the shadows, she sighed, picked up her bag and shopping packages and went toward the doors to the guest house. She opened one, stepped inside and shut it behind her.

Chapter Twenty

Jack lay on his bed in the dark room, one arm behind his head, the other resting on his stomach a few inches from his erect penis, which throbbed and strained at the front of his shorts.

The red numerals on the electric clock on the bedside table read zero two hundred hours, and he swore. He hadn't slept a wink since he'd gone to bed.

The reason? He couldn't clear his mind of images of Sarah lying alone in the guest house, waiting for him. No other woman had ever aroused him as much as she did and it was driving him crazy.

Thoughts of her slim naked body, lovely eyes and the way she swiped her tongue along her lips when she was turned on was trigger enough for him to want to play with his cock and seek his own release. He was close to giving himself a hand job, which was something he hadn't done since he was an adolescent.

The much more appealing alternative was to creep out into the night like a lovesick teenager, go to Sarah and make love to her.

Jack's balls pulsed with a sympathetic ache, and he groaned and sat up. He shifted uncomfortably, adjusted himself and rose to go toward the window.

He had left the drapes open to let in the moonlight and he could see the small building where she was whenever he looked out, which had amounted to at least half a dozen times since he'd retired to bed.

Jack folded his arms and stared at the guest house, his gaze locking on to a golden radiance which flooded out through a six-inch gap in the drapes.

She's waiting for me.

Her shadow glided behind the heavy material and his cock throbbed. The pain of need twisted in his gut like a knife.

His patience was wearing thin, his control over his actions lessening as each minute passed. His balls hurt and his penis ached for a woman he was desperate to have. His heart craved the woman who could give him everything if he let her.

Fuck. Fuck. Fuck.

Jack couldn't spend the night without her. He grabbed his pants from a chair and pulled them on, being extra careful when he tucked himself away. He found a zip-up sweatshirt, dragged it on and put up the hood before he thrust his feet into the leather moccasins that rested beneath his bed.

He was careful to avoid creaky oak floorboards as he crossed the room and went to the door. When he reached it, he turned the handle and pulled it open.

The moon's rays flooded in through the stained-glass window at the end of the hallway and illuminated him when he stepped from the room. He was eager to get going, and he hurried to the top of the stairs and stopped.

He held his breath and listened for any noise in the house. He heard a faint thud from somewhere on the ground floor, but when the noise wasn't repeated, he hurried down the stairs. His heart pounded because, in a few minutes, he would be with Sarah.

He knew he was acting like a teenager in a hormonal tangle over a girl, but he felt exhilarated and, for the first time in his life, alive. He couldn't believe he was reduced to caring for and wanting a woman so much that he would risk throwing aside not only his career but also his hard-won status in the naval community. When he thought about her or was in her presence, logic vanished and his common sense went with it.

Jack crossed the entrance hall toward the kitchen and was about to enter the shadowy room and head for the exit to the backyard when he heard a faint noise from his father's study.

He stopped dead in his tracks and spun around. He noticed lamplight pooling on the floor through the door, which was ajar, and he walked quietly to the room. He peered through the gap and saw his dad pacing the carpet and heard him muttering under his breath and reading from a sheet of paper. Jack pushed the door open wide enough for him to enter.

"Hey, Dad," he greeted, his voice low so he wouldn't wake the entire household, "you're up late."

Stewart raised his head on hearing his son and smiled. "Jack. What are *you* doing up?"

"Couldn't sleep. Doing anything interesting?"

Stewart waved the paper in the air. "Your mom got pissed at my damn speech which, I might add, I'd already written. She ordered me to get rid of the rude bits and the jokes. I don't know why, but she hates my funnies. It reads pretty boring now, but if it makes her happy, it'll save my skin."

Jack laughed. "Need any help with it?" he asked, hoping his offer would be declined.

"Nope. I'm good. But thanks."

There was a small silence then Stewart asked, "You going somewhere?"

"Out for a walk," Jack replied.

Stewart's voice was casual when he said, "Yeah, I used to do that a lot when I met your mom. The hoodie looks good though. Covert ops?"

"Yeah. Thought I'd stay in the shadows in case mom sees me and freaks out."

"Uh-huh. I did that as well when I was dating your mom."

Jack understood what his father was hinting at but didn't rise to the bait. "Goodnight, Dad. Don't stay up too late."

As Jack turned to leave, Stewart stopped him. "Jack?"

Jack glanced over his shoulder and cocked an eyebrow questioningly.

"I know you haven't got where you are by being stupid and irresponsible, and you're a mature man with a brain in your head," Stewart said. "Sarah is gorgeous and she's intelligent, with a great personality. But she's young, so be careful. You've got a lot to lose."

Jack grinned uneasily. "I will. Goodnight, Dad."

On that note and desperate to be gone, he left the room. He hurried to the kitchen and greeted Miss Fortune when the retriever raised her noble head at his entrance.

He strode to the door, fumbled with the bolt and let himself out. He crossed the veranda, jumped down the steps and broke into a jog on a heading toward the guest house, skirting the marquee in his path as he went.

He breathing was rapid when he reached his destination, and it wasn't from his increased pace.

He didn't want to frighten Sarah or wake her if she was sleeping—although he might forgo the latter because he was so turned on. Butterflies had materialized in his solar plexus and his heart, adrenaline coursed through his veins and the back of his neck, and the base of his spine prickled.

Jack peered through the six-inch gap in the drapes. His legs went weak and his cock strained against the front of his jeans.

Sarah was dancing, and when he listened hard, he could hear music playing in the room. Her hips swayed provocatively and she rotated them in small erotic circles, reminiscent of her movements when they'd made love. She moved her arms sinuously like a dancer's, flexing her hands and fingers and curling them sensuously.

But it was what she was wearing that made Jack's heart pound and sent his blood pressure soaring. The sight made his balls and penis hurt so much that he groaned through clenched teeth.

She wore a delicate all-over-lace robe in burgundy with a soft satin tie emphasizing her tiny waist. The garment fell to the tops of her thighs, had wide kimono-style sleeves and floated around her.

It was also see-through. Her femininely muscled bottom flexed, and when she turned, he saw that her nipples—which he'd tasted only the previous night and this morning—were erect and pushing at the light fabric.

"Holy. Fucking. Shit," he muttered.

I'm fucking screwed and I don't give a flying fuck.

Jack couldn't take any more. He thought his cock was going to explode and his balls implode with how tight they'd become—even before he'd had a chance to touch her.

To alert her to his presence, he tapped on the door then pushed it open and stepped inside. It swung shut behind him and he waited impatiently for her to notice his presence.

Sarah must have sensed he was behind her because she whirled to face him. Her robe drifted up to the tops of her thighs, giving him a glimpse of the dark hair between her legs.

She licked her lower lip, leaving it as moist and slick as a ripe raspberry, and her gaze traveled to his groin. She must have noticed his hardness because she walked slowly toward him, hips swaying, breasts rising and falling with each step.

Jack growled, and in a moment of sanity, thought he sounded like a wild animal. He hurried to meet her, grabbed her on either side of her waist and lifted her. He carried her to the wall beside the bed, set her on her feet and pushed her against the hard surface.

"I'm going to fuck you senseless," he said in a voice that was deep and labored with sexual meaning.

Chapter Twenty-One

Sarah lost her breath. His words were crude and unexpected and they set her on fire. Wetness dampened the insides of her thighs and the tingling pressure made her gasp for air.

Jack rested his hands on either side of her head and searched first down then up her body. At last he raised his eyes to hers and his gaze held a frightening intensity, as if he wanted to devour her in one touch. Sexual tension crackled between them and she became overwhelmingly aroused. Heat swarmed around her neck and into her cheeks, her pulse raced and her heart pounded so hard that she felt faint.

He knows. He knows what I'm thinking. He knows I want him to fuck me and his being near me is driving me insane.

Still with his palms pressed flat on the wall, Jack slammed his mouth into hers, and sparks exploded. Sexual awareness traveled through Sarah straight to her core and carnal exhilaration hit her so hard that her knees nearly gave way.

She moaned and he put his arms around her waist. She had no time to enjoy the kick of lust in her belly because he seized her hips and hauled her onto her toes.

Jack kissed her face and neck before returning to her mouth, where he ravaged her with his tongue, she in turn whimpering at its invasion.

She swayed a little under the gust of heat that enveloped her and clutched his shoulders to steady herself. She aligned her body to his and pulled his head toward her so that his lips pressed harder to hers.

His touch burned through the lace of her robe to her skin and she closed her eyes and drank in the feel of him. He tightened his grip on her until she felt both pain and pleasure and she wanted his skin against hers, so she moved her hands from the back of his neck and unknotted the satin belt at her waist.

Without releasing her mouth, Jack tore the garment from her body. He let it drop to the floor, leaving her standing before him, proud in her nakedness.

He unerringly found her breasts and cupped them. He pulled and squeezed them and flicked her nipples, then teased them with his thumbs.

Sarah moaned softly and she reached for the front of his jeans. She unfastened the button, unzipped him and pushed them downward far enough that he could kick them off.

She pulled his shorts away from his belly and his dick sprang free, hard and rigid and hot. Jack gasped when Sarah touched him. He bucked his hips so that his cock prodded at the wet curls between her thighs, and she grasped him and ran her thumb over the glans.

Jack drew his fingertips down her stomach before he buried them in the wetness between her legs. One of his fingers bared her to his touch and he teased her folds.

He rubbed her in a circular pattern and Sarah yelped. Reality and sexual desire collided then exploded into a turmoil of sensation. Tension built in her muscles and she suddenly fell over the edge into her orgasm. A shattering pleasure made her cry out her release against his mouth.

His assault of her body continued. He inserted a second finger inside her entrance and thrust them into her as though they were an extension of his penis.

Still reeling from her climax, Sarah undid his hoodie and shoved it from his shoulders and arms, letting it fall to the floor.

She drew her mouth back from his and sucked at the damp, hot flesh of his neck, then nuzzled his skin and kissed his left shoulder. She circled her tongue in small, ever-widening swirls along the firm muscle before she sucked and nipped him hard with her teeth.

Jack inserted his cock between her legs, not entering her but moving himself over her clit in a slow and delicious rhythm.

He unerringly found her G-spot with his fingers and thrust back and forth while she trailed her fingernails down his spine until she could cup his firm, sculptured buttocks, which tightened at her touch.

Sarah slid her hands from his bottom up to his back. When she felt his powerful muscles flex and contract, her skin tingled in reaction to the unleashed strength under her palms.

Jack groaned and pulled her into his body. She quivered, closed her eyes and waited in anticipation for his kiss. When he crushed his mouth on hers — lips fierce and eager and bruising in their forcefulness — she melted against him.

He entwined his tongue with hers and Sarah drank in his essence as if she were starving for him and he was the only one who could quench her thirst.

Intense heat coiled in her belly and spread outward until she felt that if Jack didn't make love to her, she would be consumed in a burning conflagration of his making. She tossed her head and uttered encouraging soft sighs and whimpers to hasten their lovemaking.

Jack left her mouth and kissed her neck and shoulder, leaving a scalding trail across her skin. Volcanic shivers rippled through her and Sarah knew she was going to climax once more.

He withdrew his fingers from her and his rigid and unyielding penis took their place, pushing at her cleft. He ground his hips painfully against hers and roamed his hands up her spine to the back of her head, where he clenched his fingers in her hair.

He pulled his dick from her entrance and Sarah massaged the muscles of his abdomen, feeling them contract at her touch. She trailed her fingers to his rigid cock and grasped him firmly while, with her other hand, she cupped his balls.

Jack placed his hand over hers, staying her movement. She let him go, sensing he was on the brink of losing control.

Without warning, he took hold of his penis, bent his knees and thrust the engorged tip into her, quick and hard.

Sexual excitement gripped Sarah and she gasped. He slipped ever deeper into her and she welcomed him, her slick, tight heat aiding him to glide in until he could go no farther.

He uttered small grunts and groans as he moved in tiny plunges, as if he only had tenuous self-control.

Their mouths met, tongues curling in heated passion, and Sarah gripped his shoulders as he kissed her. Jack's pace quickened and his movements became powerful and hard.

He held her in a vise-like grip beneath his onslaught. He pummeled her with long measured strokes and a single-minded purpose, and their bodies slapped together, creating a delicious sound.

The movement of his tongue matched his cock's rhythm and, with familiar exquisite feelings spiraling and peaking, Sarah's moans and whimpers grew louder. As if he sensed she was going to climax, Jack's thrusts grew harder and faster.

Sarah's orgasm exploded. She tensed, almost screamed and dug her fingernails into his muscles. Jack shouted something unintelligible and thrust into her one final time before he came.

She clung to him, heart pounding and her legs threatening to give way under her. Jack caught her to him, hugged her tight and kissed her face and neck tenderly.

Her body quivered in reaction to their intense lovemaking and she nuzzled her face into the warm skin of his shoulder while he stroked her spine.

They stood pressed together for some time before Sarah regained enough of her composure to raise her head to stare into Jack's face. His gaze caught hers and he smiled.

"You okay?" he asked.

Sarah nodded and returned his smile. "Nearly," she replied and kissed his mouth.

"We should get some sleep. You look all in."

Sarah laughed out loud. "I wonder why."

Jack kissed her forehead.

"Are you staying?" she asked shyly.

"Try stopping me," Jack answered and released her from his arms. In a swift movement, he picked her up and walked the short distance to the bed, where he laid her on the comforter. He went to the other side and drew back the linen.

"Rack time," he said and got under the covers.

Sarah scooted backward then turned to face him and lay down. He was lying in the same position, and when she rested her hand between them, he took hers in his and kissed each finger. They gazed at each other silently for a few moments, and the corner of his mouth lifted in his trademark lopsided grin.

"You're gonna kill me," he said.

Sarah smiled. "I doubt that."

They fell silent and she yawned.

Jack laughed. "And so endeth the conversation."

"Sorry. I think I'm about to fall into a sex-induced coma."

Jack kissed her lingeringly on the mouth. "Yeah. Right. Roll over. I'm partial to getting as close as I can to your extremely delectable butt."

A shiver of residual sexual desire ran through Sarah's limbs but she obeyed. He curved his body around hers, put a hand on her waist and pulled her in tight to him.

"Goodnight," he whispered.

Sarah wanted to tell him what she'd known from the very start—that she loved him. She knew it was too soon and he might not be ready to hear her say it. If fate stepped in, he never would be. He hadn't given her a sign that he felt anything for her other than a sexual attraction.

The thought made her a little sad, but she quickly dismissed the feeling, snuggled into his warmth and said, "Goodnight," with all the love she could infuse into her voice.

Chapter Twenty-Two

Sarah awoke, and with her eyes half-open, she stretched languidly beneath the comforter. There was a pleasurable soreness between her thighs and her breasts were tender, evidence she'd been handled roughly by a man—her man.

The memory of her and Jack making love with a passion she'd not known existed, or could have imagined, penetrated her mind. The thoughts sent tremors through her and she hugged herself.

Jack's body warmth, which she'd become familiar with and needed, was absent and she scooted backward and slid into coldness. The space beside her was empty and she sat up, searched the room and saw that he was gone.

She had no idea what time he'd left, so she must have been exhausted not to have sensed him leaving. With some trepidation, she glanced at her watch to see that it was ten hundred hours. While everyone else was embroiled in arrangements for the wedding, she'd slept unforgivably late, and it made her feel guilty and embarrassed.

Shit.

She sat on the edge of the bed and ran her fingers through her tangled hair. She glanced toward the doors to see if the drapes were still closed and she sighed with relief. They were, and nobody in the yard could see her if they passed by the guest house.

Sarah glanced down at her body and saw that Jack had left his mark on her nakedness. Small rosy areas marred her skin — legacy of his possession — with one or two darker hues surrounded by faint teeth impressions, proof that his passion had gotten the better of him.

She ran her fingertip over one and her heart fluttered with the knowledge that she was his, and as far as she was concerned, she would always be.

Her nipples hardened and a familiar ache coalesced in her stomach. To distract her mind, she gazed around the large room, admiring the peach and cream décor with its floral drapes, matching bed linen and luxurious wall-to-wall carpet.

There were two doors that opened off the main room, one to a wet room and the other to a walk-in closet.

Her thoughts backtracked and she remembered how Jack had made love to her with a strength and power borne of his need for her. Her body flushed with heat when she recollected how she had been so desperately hungry for him.

She trailed her hand across the rumpled sheets on which he'd slept, and she sighed.

I love him.

The confession didn't surprise her, as she'd already admitted it to herself. It did make her a little sad, because there were several obstacles standing in the way of their being together, the primary one — which appeared insurmountable — being their careers.

Sarah mentally shook herself and glanced at the bedside table. She stared at what had been placed there and smiled.

Jack had returned sometime during the morning while she'd slept, because he'd left a breakfast tray for her. A small, slim crystal vase had been placed in the center and contained a single red rose. There was a glass of orange juice and a plate with a lid. When she lifted it, she found pancakes doused in syrup, and her mouth watered.

Sarah covered the food, touched the bloom's delicate petals and stroked their velvety softness. A surge of love swept through her at his thoughtfulness.

She was about to turn away when she noticed a folded piece of paper propped against the decorative container. She picked it up and opened it.

A murmured "Oh," escaped her when she read its contents.

Sarah,

Mom is acting demented and I've been summoned for duty to keep her in line. It's Dad's last wish before he kills her. I didn't want to wake you so I snuck out. You look like an angel when you're asleep, by the way. I've left you breakfast. Enjoy it and chill out. I'll be back later when I've been dismissed.

Thank you for one of the best nights of my life.

Jack x

Sarah read the note once more, folded it and pressed it to her heart.

I love you, Jack.

She had no idea when he would return, so she quickly did justice to the food, removed the vase from the tray and placed it on a side table then went in search of her sea bag.

Once she'd found it, she took out her toiletries and towel from its depths and entered the wet room, locking the door behind her. She showered quickly, stepped out, dried herself and wound her towel turban-like around her head before she went into the bedroom.

She dressed in a night shirt and sat to dry her hair, brushing the tresses vigorously once she'd finished and pulling the long strands into a high ponytail. She put on jeans and a tight white T-shirt and thrust her feet into her flat shoes.

Ready for Jack's return, she straightened the pillows and comforter, breathing in the faint musky odor of their lovemaking, which drifted up from the crisp linen.

Her task complete, Sarah went to the drapes and pulled them aside, letting in the sunlight. Through the glass, she could see a depthless blue sky and brilliant green grass bordered by the deeper green, silvers and browns of the forest.

It was a glorious day for a wedding and an equally beautiful one to be in love. She opened the doors and breathed the pine and woody scent that drifted in.

From the direction of the marquee she heard voices, and she smiled, because ringing out above them all were Wendy's strident tones as she ordered everyone about.

Sarah turned, walked to the bed and sat herself on its edge. She didn't know what she should do — go find Jack, help with the arrangements or wait where she was.

She was saved from making a final decision when she heard a soft tap. She turned to see him standing at the open door and she smiled in delight. She hurried toward him and, in seconds, she was in his arms.

He held her tight and kissed her face and neck with small heated kisses, then he captured her mouth and proceeded to kiss her so thoroughly that she couldn't catch her breath.

She clung to him as if they'd been apart for days instead of hours.

Jack drew back and grinned. "Whoa," he said. "That was some welcome. Can we do a run through?"

Sarah's face flushed. "Count yourself lucky. I'm normally a grump in the mornings."

"I can't say I've noticed," Jack replied. "I've been pretty distracted myself."

His voice deepened, his eyes darkened and Sarah's knees went weak. His gaze was warm and so intense as he stared at her that she felt he was undressing her with his eyes.

Her face burned with a fiery blush and she squirmed with the delicious sensations that he was invoking in her.

"I've finally been dismissed. Want to go for a walk?"

Sarah dismissed her licentious thoughts and smiled. "I'd love to, but doesn't your mother need help?"

"I wouldn't go there. She's murder to be around right now, so we should stay out of her way for a while."

Jack took her hand and Sarah entwined her fingers with his. They went out into the garden and he led her across the grass toward a narrow dirt path that disappeared into the forest, worn away by many feet over time.

Once they'd set foot on the dusty track, they wound their way through umber-brown and dark green trees that reeked of age. The air was redolent with an aroma of woody incense from centuries of snapping branches that had crashed to the forest floor and rotted silently amid the undergrowth.

Sunlight streamed through gnarled branches twisted together overhead and dappled the green-speckled trunks. The rays pooled on the ground and swarmed among the piled vegetation in streaks of antique gold.

A bird chorus was loud and tuneful and dried leaves crunched under their feet while their footwear kicked dust into clouds in the still air.

Sarah peeked sideways at Jack and smiled secretly at his muscular physique in a khaki T-shirt and the way his torn and faded jeans clung to his thighs and bottom.

As she stared in what she thought was a surreptitious way at his backside as it shifted eye-catchingly beneath the denim material, Jack elbowed her.

"Are you eyeing my butt, Lieutenant?" he asked.

"Busted," Sarah said and laughed out loud. "It's a cute one though, Captain."

Jack tightened his grip on her hand. "Cute? Great. Now I've heard everything."

They didn't speak for some time, but it wasn't an uncomfortable silence. They were at ease in each other's company, and even though sexual tension crackled between them, words were unnecessary.

It wasn't until the path ended and Sarah gasped at the sight before her that the silence was broken.

They stood in a small glade with the forest spreading out on either side to encircle a large pond. The ground sloped gently to green water that was dotted with yellow and white lilies set in the center of heart-shaped leaves.

Swirls curdled the tranquil, mirror-like surface as fish breached, birds swooped backward and forward across its expanse and iridescent blue and green dragonflies darted about in a dance of life.

"It's beautiful," Sarah said and turned to stare at Jack, who was watching her intently.

Captured by his gaze, which seemed to be offering her so much, Sarah grew still.

"So are you," he said and pulled her toward him.

Sarah went to him eagerly and put her arms around his neck. As if he were starving for her, Jack's mouth met hers and he kissed her with such an intense passion that Sarah wondered if she would ever be able to survive without him.

He gripped her backside, and she felt his ready erection and squirmed against it. He thrust his tongue into her mouth and her moans sent the birds soaring from the tree tops.

Still kissing her, Jack guided her away from the open space and backward against a tree trunk so she was supported by the wood. He bent his knees and his restrained cock pushed between her legs at her entrance.

He grazed her bottom lip with sensual possessive-ness and Sarah returned it by biting his. Her mouth burned when his lips touched hers and she whimpered as he forcefully pressed his hips against hers, as if he would enter her through the denim.

Sarah wanted him to take her right there, regardless of whether they could be seen by anyone approaching along the path. She couldn't get enough of the man who had awakened every erotic thought and feeling she possessed in her body.

He was like a drug she couldn't give up. He was emotion and sensation, which left her wanting more, and he was love, which filled her and swamped her soul.

She was therefore left wanting when he drew away from her and bowed his head. He was shaking and his breathing was ragged. She touched his hip to calm him.

He rested a hand on the tree trunk above her head, opened his eyes and cupped her face in his palm. His caressed her skin with his fingers and grinned. "What the hell have you done to me?" he said. "I can't stop thinking about you for a second and it's impossible to keep my hands to myself when you're near me."

Sarah's stomach lurched, and she rested both palms on his chest and felt the strong beat of his heart beneath them.

"You're the only woman who's ever gotten under my skin," he continued. "I need you with me so badly."

"Jack," Sarah said softly and tilted her head to increase the pressure of his hand on her face.

Jack took a deep breath. "Sarah, I I—"

"Eeewww, get a room, you two."

A teasing female voice stopped Jack. His body tensed and he stepped backward. An irritated expression crossed his face and he turned to his sister. "You shouldn't creep up on people like that, Hayley," he said, a slight edge to his tone.

"Well, darn me. Have I interrupted something?" Hayley asked. "Sorry, big brother, but Mom has sent me to summon you. Dad is freaking out about something trivial, so you have to come."

With her message safely delivered, Hayley retraced her steps, leaving Jack and Sarah in a silence fraught with unfulfilled desire and something else.

He took her hand in his and, in silence, they returned along the path. Sarah glanced at him and noticed his jaw was set and a muscle spasmed under his skin. His eyes were distant, and when they exited the trees, he turned to her and kissed her.

"I'll be back for you at fourteen hundred hours," he said.

He traced her lips with his finger, smiled and left, leaving Sarah to wonder why he suddenly appeared so unapproachable.

She made her way toward the guest house and, feeling very much on her own, she opened the door and went inside.

Chapter Twenty-Three

Sarah studied herself in the full-length mirror and wondered if her dress was suitable for a wedding. Fashion lines had changed drastically in recent times but she was unsure whether she was overdressed.

She half-turned to peruse her bottom in the tight skirt and looked at herself critically one last time.

The dusky pink suited her coloring. The plunging neckline was not so low that she feared her breasts would be exposed for all the guests to see. The wide shoulder straps held the bodice in place and had the same lace applique that covered the upper part of the garment to her waist, divided at each hip and ran down to the hem, which rested a few inches above her knees.

The material clung to her curves, emphasizing the swell of her hips and outlining the feminine muscles in her thighs. Her high-heeled stiletto shoes made the best of her legs and there was no need for her to wear pantyhose, as she already sported a golden tan.

Sarah had arranged her hair meticulously, piling it into loose curls atop her head and fastening it in place with glittering bobby pins. She had purchased a pink crystal barrette, which she used at the base of her up-do as added reinforcement in case her styling skills proved to be as dismal as they'd always been.

Before dressing, she'd rubbed lotion into her body, and her skin now gleamed like silk. She'd sprayed perfume on her most exposed and intimate areas, hoping Jack would seek them out later. The final accessories to her ensemble were delicate crystal stud earrings and a necklace and bracelet of the same design.

Sarah checked her makeup, and when she was as satisfied as she could be with her appearance, stepped away from the mirror and collected her pocketbook to look through its contents. She confirmed she had everything she needed and walked to the doors, opened the drapes and checked to see if Jack was on his way.

There was no sign of him and she bit her bottom lip, immediately regretting doing so, because she tasted lip gloss. She was eager to see him and the few hours away from him had made her impatient.

As she paced the bedroom, she checked her watch frequently, only to see that single minutes had passed since the last time she'd looked. Finally, she went to the doors once again to see if there was any sign of him.

The instant she looked out, she saw him walking toward her, dressed in his white uniform and wearing his cap. She thought how he dominated his environment and, more importantly, how gracefully he moved for such a tall man and how devastatingly sexy he was.

He caught sight of her and grinned, but it vanished when he drew close to the guest house. She opened a door and went out to meet him, her own smile wide and happy.

Jack stopped a few feet from her and his gaze roamed her body. "Wow," was his only greeting.

"Is this okay?" Sarah asked nervously. "Does it cover everything it's supposed to? It's not too over-the-top?"

"Holy shit, yeah," Jack said. "I mean, yes, yes and no, it's not." He stepped forward and smiled. "You're stunning."

He clasped her hand and tucked it into his arm. "Shall we go take our seats?"

Sarah nodded and they walked to where an area for the wedding ceremony had been set up alongside the marquee.

She eagerly took in the scene as they got nearer. White wooden chairs had been arranged in rows on each side of a narrow white carpet to create an aisle. Tied into large bows around the seat backs were shimmering white chiffon sashes decorated with small posies of blue, yellow and white flowers, finished off with slender green ferns.

An arch had been placed at the end of the aisle where the couple were to take their vows. It too was festooned in the same sheer cloth and adorned with clusters of the same color blooms as the chairs.

Petals of the same hues had been strewn along the carpet, and swathes of sheer drapery, again decorated with bunches of sweet-smelling blossoms, ran along its edges.

The marquee had been decorated in corresponding colors and the sides had been gathered and fastened to the eaves so Sarah was able to see a wooden dance floor inside, with discotheque equipment set up ready for the night's entertainment.

Small, round tables with seating, available for the guests to eat and drink at, were displayed inside the tent, all draped in the glistening chiffon with more flowers arranged in tall crystal vases as centerpieces.

Sarah's eyes fell on the guests who milled about the yard and nerves kick-started in her stomach. She must have hesitated, because Jack turned to her, a questioning expression on his face.

"Is something wrong?" he asked.

Sarah frowned. "I'm not sure…this is a good idea, Jack," she said. "What if someone here knows you…us?"

"We'll deal with it. You're with me. That's what counts. Forget it and relax. Okay?"

He drew her forward and her mouth went dry as they approached a crowd of what looked to be approximately a hundred people.

Jack inclined his head to some guests when they greeted him and Sarah noticed many staring at her. Nerves jangled inside her but she raised her chin, determined to enjoy herself by being with the man beside her.

Jack guided Sarah away from the men and women and took her to the rows of chairs on the left side of the aisle. She tried to withdraw her hand from his arm so she could sit behind him in the second row as wedding etiquette depicted, but he stopped her and frowned.

"Where do you think you're going?" he asked.

"To sit in the second row," Sarah replied. "Only you, your mom and dad and grandparents should sit —"

Jack shook his head before she'd completed her sentence. "Forget it. You sit with me."

He led her onward and indicated a chair halfway along the first row. She seated herself and he sat beside her.

"Let's get one thing straight, Sarah," he said. "You're here with me and that's how I want it. You'll get to know that I'm a stubborn son of a bitch and always get want I want...eventually."

Jack softened his statement by stroking her palm with his thumb, which sent shocks of pleasure coursing through her arm. She licked her lips in response to the sensation.

"Yes, sir," she replied, teasing him. "Whatever you say, Captain."

"Okay. That's a bit over the top, but...we'll see about *that* tonight."

Sarah wriggled on the hard seat and she stared into his eyes. "We certainly will, sir."

Jack surreptitiously adjusted the front of his pants. "Shit," he murmured. "Christ, Sarah. Let's save this conversation for later, shall we?"

Anticipation stirred inside her and she tried to slow her heart, which was racing at breakneck speed, and concentrate on the scene playing out around her.

* * * *

The wedding began on time and appeared to go without a hitch. Sarah was transfixed throughout the ceremony as she took in the handsome groom in his blue Navy dress uniform and the bride looking effervescent in her white lace, strapless, fishtail dress with three attendants in buttercup yellow chiffon gowns standing by their escorts, who were also in uniform.

The sun shone on the euphoric couple and the birds sang in harmony with the hymns, as if they too were happy and in love. The groom nearly dropped the ring, but in a series of acrobatic moves saved it. Everyone laughed, including Ashleigh.

Their vows were their own, and when Sarah heard the poignant words uttered with such love and meaning behind them, her heart ached with a strange yearning.

She'd attended a few weddings in the past, but had never felt so emotional about such an event as she did then.

The ceremony at an end, Ashleigh and her new husband returned down the aisle to rousing cheers and thunderous clapping. They went off to have official photographs taken and Jack rose, along with the other guests, and pulled Sarah to her feet. He drew her hand through his arm once more and murmured in her ear, "I need a drink."

They joined the people heading toward the bar arranged inside the marquee and Jack grabbed two mimosas from a waiter. The master of ceremonies eventually summoned the guests for photographs, and in between sipping their champagne and orange juice cocktails, Sarah found herself having to run backward and forward with Jack to pose with groups of family and friends.

She'd been unwilling to join the wedding party for pictures and had let Jack know of her reluctance. He'd insisted, however, with a firmness that had brought the heat to her face, that she go with him.

With her hand clasped in his and his arm touching hers, she felt more buoyant and hopeful for their future. She decided that the only thing that mattered was the here and now and she was going to exist in the moment.

After some time, the emcee called the guests to the marquee, where everyone found their respective seats, all of which were labeled with place cards stating their names.

Once everybody was seated, there was a loud fanfare played by the discotheque and the newly married couple entered the marquee to loud and raucous applause. There was no top table and they seated themselves at a small, intimate one in the center of the dance floor. The one for the parents and an even larger one for the attendants and their escorts had been placed in a circle around them.

Sarah was surprised when Jack led her to their own table alongside the bridesmaids, confirmation that the Chalmers family did acknowledge who she was and wanted her there. It was a sentiment to be cherished.

Jack held Sarah's chair out for her, and once she'd made herself comfortable, he sat next to her. He kept a proprietorial hand on her leg, as if he wasn't concerned that it might be noticed, and she wondered if he had thrown caution to the winds and no longer cared if their relationship became common knowledge.

The official speeches were rude — as expected — and hilarious from the father of the bride and heartfelt from anyone else who wanted to speak. The meal ranged over five courses and was delicious, and the tent buzzed with animated conversation and rang with laughter as the guests consumed more liquor and conventional inhibitions were tossed by the wayside.

The sky grew dusky with evening and the lights strung in the trees and in and outside the marquee were switched on. Lanterns had been hung from the branches and on stakes dug into the ground, illuminating a grassy path to the house so no one could wander off and become lost in the woods or take an impromptu swim in the lake.

Once the meal was finished, some of the tables and chairs were moved from the floor and taken outside to enable people to enjoy the warm air and so the staff managing the discotheque could erect the remainder of their equipment.

This was done in record time and Ashleigh and her new husband, who Sarah had found out was named Jake, stepped onto the floor and performed their wedding dance.

The parents took to the floor for the next tune and the bridesmaids with their escorts joined in halfway through. Toward the end, everyone congregated around them and the music ended in cheers and ribald comments as the night's entertainment commenced.

The first song for the guests announced its arrival with a thunderous roll of drums, and everyone whistled and clapped. Sarah smiled at Jack, feeling his touch burn through the material of her dress, and she tried to ignore the sensations he was stirring in her.

She hoped he would ask her to dance, but if he didn't, she didn't care, because it was enough to be with him.

Her attention was diverted when Stewart appeared at her side. "Come on, Sarah. Let's show 'em how it's done."

Sarah grinned, glanced at Jack before he pulled her from her chair and onto the floor. He spun her before clasping her around the waist and holding her tightly.

He then whirled her in a series of flashy Spanish-type steps and she tossed her head back and laughed with delight.

Chapter Twenty-Four

Jack watched Sarah being pulled away by his father and let his breath out in a gust, as if he'd been holding it in for some time.

Once she started to dance, he couldn't take his eyes off her. He stared at her rounded bottom and the way she shimmied her hips and sashayed in her moves. Muscles flexed sinuously in her long, slim legs and he remembered those same limbs clenching his hips to pull his cock in deeper.

He understood why he couldn't keep his eyes and his hands off her. She was all woman — sweet and childlike but damned sexy and provocative.

His penis stirred and hardened and he quickly dismissed the image from his mind. She laughed each time his dad spun her. His heart pounded unevenly and a damp sweat broke out along his spine and on his forehead.

Jack wiped his face and tried to calm himself. He was fighting a losing battle, and given his present state and at the first opportunity, he was going to take Sarah to the guest house and make love to her.

Ashleigh sat in Sarah's chair and smiled at him, distracting him from his thoughts. Jack forced his traitorous mind into some semblance of order. "You look gorgeous, Ash."

His grin was as natural as he could make it and he stretched out his hand to grasp his sister's slim one.

Ashleigh squeezed his fingers and returned his smile. "It's been the best day of my life, Jack — even more so because you're here."

She stared at him for a few moments, then Ashleigh withdrew from their physical contact. She was quiet for a moment then said in a rush, "You're in love with Sarah."

It was a statement of fact, not a question, and Jack jerked in surprise. His mouth twisted in a grimace. *How did she guess?*

"I am?" he asked, playing it cool.

"You are," Ashleigh echoed.

Jack cleared his throat. "I guess now that you're married, you're an authority on love and relationships?"

"No, I'm not, big brother. It's written all over your face and, anyway, I'm your sister. I love you and I know you."

"Go on."

"Your eyes follow her around like a lovesick puppy. You bristle each time you see a man look at her. You've changed, as well. You laugh more, you're relaxed and not as unapproachable as you used to be."

"Uh-huh. You've managed to assassinate my character and destroy my self-image. I won't ever feel the same way about myself again." Jack laughed out loud and tried to make a joke of his sister's descriptive tearing apart of his badass veneer. More importantly, he tried to turn the subject away from her intuitive statement that he was in love with Sarah.

While the idea didn't shock him, because he'd nearly confessed his true feelings to her when they'd been at the lake that afternoon, the reality of someone pointing it out to him had rocked him.

"Sarah loves *you* as well," Ashleigh went on, and Jack knew she wasn't going to be swayed from what she wanted to say.

Jack felt a sensation akin to being punched in the gut. "She does?"

"Oh, my Lord, Jack, you're so exasperating. Why do you have to ask a question every time I say something?"

Jack ignored his sister's frustration. "How do you know?"

"Seriously? Are you blind? She has the same problem as you. She can't keep her eyes off you. It's embarrassing. She lights up when you're near her and, anyway, women can always tell things like that about another woman."

Jack's tone was sarcastic. "Oh, yeah, the female thing."

Ashleigh laughed at Jack's cynicism. "Yes. The woman thing. It's always right on. Trust me."

Jack was shell-shocked at his sister's disclosure that Sarah was in love with him. The neck of his tunic suddenly felt too tight and he ran a finger inside it to loosen it.

He was choosing his words carefully to continue the conversation when his father delivered Sarah to her chair, bowing in an old-fashioned manner before leaving her.

Jack grinned at her flushed appearance.

"Your father is quite the mover," Sarah said and wrinkled her pert nose at him. "He nearly wore me out."

Jack was about to speak when the music started to play again and Ashleigh rose to her feet.

"You think my dad has some moves? Wait till you see our Jack's."

Jack shook his head and looked horrified. "Oh, hell no."

Ashleigh walked to his side and grabbed his hand. "Oh, hell yes. Don't be an ass," she said and pulled him from his seat onto the dance floor.

Sarah sat on the seat vacated by Jack and watched as he went reluctantly with his sister. She laughed when Hayley joined them and the women went to stand on each side of him to trap him between them so he couldn't make an escape.

When he began to dance, she was disconcerted to see that he was able to move extremely well. He kept perfect time with the beat, his moves sexy and fluid. He flexed his broad shoulders and torso gracefully but in a masculine way, and Sarah yearned to join him so she could feel his body against hers.

When she looked around the tent, she noticed women of all ages looking at the small group as well. It made her wonder if they were staring at Jack or with general interest at the siblings together.

She saw Jack take Ashleigh and Hayley's hands in his and Sarah smiled as he twirled them. They laughed and once he released them, they linked their arms through his. Brief flashes from cameras came and went periodically and some guests cheered and whistled.

Sarah's heart ached with love for him. She wanted to scream out how she felt so that everyone in the marquee and outside could hear. She couldn't, though, and she bit her lip until it hurt. When he glanced over his shoulder at her and grinned, she wanted to melt at the happy expression on his face.

She couldn't lose him. If they split, her life would never be the same. Despite that, she wouldn't allow her love to destroy his career. There had to be some way they could go on, because there *was* something between them worth fighting for. She had no idea, though, what that solution was.

She was jerked from her thoughts when the song finished and the laughing trio returned to her table.

Hayley smiled at Sarah then at Jack. "Not bad, baby boy," she said and left to mingle with the other guests.

Ashleigh kissed Jack on his cheek. "I'm going to go find my husband before he gets wasted and my night is ruined," she said and walked off, leaving him and Sarah alone.

Jack inclined his head toward the dance floor. "Do you want to dance?" he asked.

"Oh, yes," Sarah answered and placed her hand in his. He led her onto the floor.

Once there, he let her go and put his arm around her waist. He took hold of her hand, but instead of clasping it to his chest as he had during their first-ever dance, he held it out to the side.

He started to sway his hips in an exaggerated fashion and performed small shuffling steps with his feet in a Latin way. Sarah laughed, enchanted, and copied his moves.

He drew away from her and she moved toward him, and when she stepped backward from him, he followed her. Each time they came together, his body brushed hers, their hips joined in perfect synchronization, and they slipped into a rhythm that was both sexy and exhilarating.

Jack thrust his leg between hers and pushed his pelvis into her so she could feel his hips rock in time to the music. He slid his hand down to rest on her lower back and they spun together. She looked at his face and fiery heat flooded through her at the expression in his eyes.

They continued to dance, first apart then close, their lower bodies brushing and nudging each other, resulting in a waxing and waning friction that had Sarah wanting more.

At one point, in response to the Spanish-sounding music, she broke away from him and pressed her palm to his chest, as if to keep him at bay. His gaze smoldered as she swayed her hips and sensually curled her body in sinuous and exotic moves.

Jack took her back into his arms and Sarah thought he kissed the side of her neck, but he pulled away from her when the track ended and she couldn't be sure.

The main lights dimmed until the only illumination came from the tea candles that burned on the tables and the twinkling lights strung around the interior.

A slow tune started to play and once more, Jack drew Sarah into his arms.

Chapter Twenty-Five

On hearing the love song made famous by a well-known romantic movie, Sarah dissolved into Jack's arms, put her own around his neck and rested the palms of her hands on the back of his head.

Jack encircled her waist with his arms and pulled her in tight to him so she could feel his thigh muscles flex and his groin push against hers. It was semi-dark in the marquee and they were hidden by shadows, and she nestled her face into his neck and kissed his warm skin.

It was difficult to remind herself where they were. They were in full view of everyone, including naval personnel, and someone might find the sight of a Navy captain in a hot clinch with his lieutenant juicy gossip. As she swayed with her man to the poignant music, Sarah didn't care. If they were going to be seen, so be it.

Jack slid his palms to her bottom then along her spine, and she rubbed herself against him. His breath was hot when he kissed her ear and her cheek and she in turn nipped at his neck and he shivered in response.

If they'd been alone, she would have begged him to take her. As it was, she could only offer him sensuous hints, using her body to make him aware that she wanted him.

Jack kissed her forehead, and when she pressed into him, she felt his erection. He bent his head toward her and his mouth was only inches from her own. The urge to kiss him was unbearable.

"I want you," he said. "Can you feel how much I want you?"

His stiff cock pressed her belly, and Sarah closed her eyes and nodded. "I want you too."

"Jesus, Sarah. This is killing me."

Jack bent his head and his mouth met hers in a kiss so forceful that it seared her lips.

She clasped the back of his neck and his hands tightened on her, his touch burning her through the material of her dress.

Sarah hadn't known how much being in love could hurt. It was a living thing gnawing away at her insides. It was both frightening and exhilarating and she was aching and heated with desire and need.

She no longer cared about rules and regulations. Given the chance, she would never let Jack go and she would love him until the day she died.

Sarah licked his lip and gently bit it. He hissed, their tongues entwined and the kiss grew frantic and hot with erotic meaning.

The song finished and they broke apart before the lights came on. They stood together on the dance floor for a few moments, their eyes locked, then Jack returned her to their table.

Still shaking from the intensity of their kiss, Sarah trailed her fingers down his arm then picked up her pocketbook.

"I have to go visit the restroom," she said.

Jack touched her hand. "Don't be long," he said and let her go. "Otherwise I'll have to come looking for you."

Sarah smiled and left the tent to make her way toward the house, preferring not to queue at the portable toilets.

As she crossed the grass, she tried to slow her racing heart and inhaled a lungful of pine-scented air. It did nothing to calm her because all she could think about was Jack.

She was nearing the veranda when someone gripped her wrist and stopped her. Startled, she turned to face a tall, slim blonde woman dressed in a dazzling crystal-studded gown with her hair in an elegant up-do.

The woman was very pretty and smiled at her in a friendly manner—however, even in the dim light, Sarah could see the gesture wasn't reflected in her eyes. She thought the stranger may have mistaken her for someone else and asked, "Can I help you?"

Sarah thought the lady looked at her in a somewhat insolent manner before she replied, "I'm Meredith Carson."

Sarah was confused. "Do I know you?"

"Jack hasn't mentioned me?"

An icy weight settled in Sarah's stomach. "Should he have?"

Meredith Carson giggled, a noise which was girlish and sounded incongruous in conjunction with her age and appearance. "Jack was always secretive regarding his personal life. I guess he hasn't changed much."

"Right," Sarah said, confusion changing to irritation. "Is there a point to this conversation?"

"You must be one of Jack's girls."

Sarah's heart lurched. She curbed an urge to tell the woman what she thought of her and said, "I tell you what, Ms. Carson. I don't know you and I don't think I want to. But I'll do you a favor. I'll go and round up Jack's other girls, we'll report to you and we can compare notes. In the meantime, I have more important business to attend to, like being with *my* man."

With that final statement, she flicked her palm in a warding off gesture and continued toward the house, her back erect and her teeth clenched.

She went through the French doors and hurried into the living room, from there going into the entrance hall. She heard loud male voices coming from the direction of the kitchen but ignored them and ascended the stairs to the restroom.

She used the facilities, washed her hands and touched up her make-up, all the while seething as to what Meredith Carson had meant, whether Jack was still dating her and, if so, how serious their relationship was or had been.

Sarah left the washroom and slowly made her way downstairs to the hall, where she decided she wanted a drink of water and made her way to the kitchen.

She stopped abruptly in the doorway when four naval officers who were leaning against or propping up the breakfast bar turned to face her. Piercing wolf whistles rent the air.

Sarah blushed and turned to leave as fast as she could. She was unceremoniously stopped from doing so when a man with a blond buzz cut hurried toward where she was standing and grasped her wrist.

"Well, hello, honey. Where have you been all my life?"

Sarah was sick and tired of being grabbed and was not amused. "Seriously?" she asked. "Give me a break. That pick-up line is as old as my grandmother."

The three other men laughed uproariously. "Looks like you're losing your touch, Andy," a dark-haired man quipped and focused his bleary gaze on Sarah. "Come on in, baby," he continued. "We can show you how charming us submariners can be."

Sarah snorted. "Thanks, but no thanks. I think I'll pass. And I'm *not* your baby."

The man called Andy squeezed her wrist. "Aww, honey. The night's young and the party is only half the fun."

Sarah wrenched her arm from the man's grip. "Please take your hand off me."

"Hey," the third man of the group said, pointing at her. "Aren't you with that old captain?"

Sarah froze and glared at him, angry heat rising to her face. "*That* old captain is worth a thousand of you."

"What the hell is going on here?"

Jack's voice came from behind her and Sarah felt his body brush her back. She heard the anger in his voice and felt the tension in his muscles.

The four officers immediately came to attention, one carefully placing his beer on the counter and moving to stand in front of it, as though to conceal it.

They didn't salute Jack but said in unison, "Sir."

Jack moved past Sarah to stand in the center of the kitchen. She watched as his gaze lingered for a few seconds on each submariner in turn.

She could see he was annoyed, because his hands were clenched into fists at his sides, and she bit her lip. She'd seen his temper before and how dangerous he'd been when he'd dealt with the man on the beach. She knew he wouldn't hold back if he thought she was in trouble, and she had no idea what the outcome of the situation here would be.

"We appear to have a problem, guys," Jack said, his voice quiet. "You see, I heard your comments and your question regarding this lady" — and he inclined his head toward Sarah — "and who she might be with here. While liquor *may*, and I say the word 'may' loosely, have played a role in your stupid-ass remarks, I'm prepared to let those slip. I do think I might be able to satisfy your curiosity as to who accompanied *Lieutenant* Morgan to this wedding. The lady happens to be with me, and if I see any of you approach her again or hear you talk to her the way you have been, I'll take each one of you to the lake, which is a little way from where we are, and kick your asses hard enough that you'll be shitting out of your mouths indefinitely. Then I'll toss you in.

"Have I made myself absolutely clear, or do you require clarification on some of the words I've used? Or perhaps you need to see an example. Does it also solve your curiosity about whether she is indeed with the *old* captain and what *this* captain can do to you if he chooses to?"

Silence reigned in the room and Sarah held her breath. Jack waited, holding his arms stiffly at his sides. She was under no illusions that he would indeed deal with the four young men in the way he'd said. Undoubtedly, he *would* throw them in the lake — and not necessarily in one piece.

It was obvious he was jealous and pissed off, but regardless of whether those emotions showed her how much he cared for her, it wasn't a good situation for a captain in the US Navy to be in.

At last, the man called Andy nodded and the others followed suit. "Perfectly understood, sir," he said. "No further clarification necessary."

"Outstanding. Let's keep it that way."

Jack about-turned and, his face set, passed Sarah, took her hand in his and led her out into the hall. They didn't speak to one another until they were out on the veranda.

There, Sarah pulled him around to face her. The question of who Meredith Carson was and what she'd meant to him had been haunting her since the woman had waylaid her.

"Who is Meredith Carson?"

Jack folded his arms, the angry expression still evident on his face. "I knew that was coming. I saw her speak to you and you didn't look too happy."

"Answer the question, Jack."

"I dated her once or twice a few years ago. She wasn't my type, but every time I came home on leave, she showed up here and wouldn't back off. In the end, I had to get nasty with her. Ashleigh thinks she still holds a torch for me, but that's her problem, not mine."

Sarah heard the sincerity in his words and relaxed. "For a minute there—"

Jack unfolded his arms and touched her lips with his finger. "You've no worries there, Sarah. There's only one woman I'm interested in and she's standing right next to me."

The silence stretched out between them. "Were you jealous...in there with those jerks?" she asked.

Jack's jaw clenched. "Nope," he answered.

Sarah smiled. "I thought you were going to kill them."

Jack looked uncomfortable. "Nope."

"Okay, but you lie so convincingly, Jack."

He suddenly took her hand and tugged her down the steps away from the veranda. She had to run as he led her past the marquee and the people standing outside.

"Where are we going?" she asked breathlessly.

"I need something," Jack replied.

"But the wedding…"

"What about it?"

"People will notice we're missing."

"Yeah? That's tough."

They reached the guest house in record time and Jack opened the door and pulled her inside. He kicked it shut behind him and pulled the curtains closed before walking to the bedside table to turn the lamp on before he faced her.

With an odd expression on his face he said, "Take off your clothes."

Sarah was stunned at his request and the way he sounded. "I don't—"

"I need a shower," he explained, interrupting her, "to cool off, and I think you do too."

Sarah hesitated. She stared at the anger that burned in his eyes then turned to stand with her back to him. "Unzip me then."

Jack touched her neck and she heard the purring noise of the fastener as he drew it downward. The garment dropped to the floor and she gracefully stepped out of it, leaving it in a pile on the rug.

She faced him and hooked her thumbs in the thin elastic of the pink lace thong she was wearing. She shimmied her hips and slowly pulled the flimsy undergarment down her legs, over her shoes then kicked the gauzy material away from her.

Except for her high-heeled shoes, she was now naked, and he raked his gaze over her body.

Her voice was low when she said, "Now you."

Jack unbuttoned his tunic and shrugged out of it, letting it fall to the floor and leaving it there. He kicked off his shoes without untying the laces, undid his pants then pushed them and his undershorts to his ankles before stepping out of them.

Sarah thought he was magnificent, all tan skin and sculptured muscle that gleamed in the warm glow bathing the room. She ran her gaze over his torso and lingered on his rigid cock, which tented the front of his shorts.

She raised her eyes to his face and he gestured at the wet room door. The air was heavy with sexual tension as Sarah obeyed his silent order and walked toward it.

She sensed Jack following her, slipped off her shoes and stepped onto the cold tiled floor.

Chapter Twenty-Six

Once inside, Sarah went to the center of the room. She stopped, half-turned and watched Jack from beneath her eyelashes as he came in behind her. He walked past her to the controls on the wall, turned the knob to the on position then waved his palm under the stream of water to test the temperature. When he appeared satisfied, he moved to stand in front of her.

Sarah stood motionless as he started to remove the bobby pins from her hair, placing each one on a glass shelf that ran the length of the room.

He never took his eyes off her, his gaze holding hers for the longest time. His stare was so intense that she shivered.

Jack withdrew the last pin, laid it beside the others and finally unclipped the barrette from the back of her up-do. It collapsed, her tresses falling in a curled mass over her shoulders, caressing her damp skin.

His hands went to either side of her head and he entwined his fingers in the thick tendrils. He massaged her scalp, his touch firm but gentle, and Sarah closed her eyes, her senses reeling from the mesmerizing motion.

"You're pretty damned amazing," he murmured.

Sarah inhaled then let her breath out slowly. She opened her eyes and looked at his face then downward to rake his glorious body.

Water glistened on his skin and his muscles curled and rippled with his movements. His erection stood straight and proud, straining toward her, and she ran a finger slowly and sensuously along his stiffness. At her touch, he grunted. He clenched his fingers in her damp mane before he cupped her face between his hands.

He leaned toward her until his mouth was inches from hers and said, "If you keep that up, I'm going to have to do something now. I want to make this last."

"Mm-m-m," Sarah said, because she didn't have an issue with him taking her right then.

Jack placed his hands on her shoulders, turned her and pushed her forward so she stood beneath the shower. The warm water pounded her head and ran in rivulets down her body. She lifted her face to the spray and relished the liquid on her hot skin.

Jack reached for something from the shelf and a moment later, with slow and languid strokes, he began to caress her spine with a soft facecloth.

His rigid cock probed her buttocks and she pushed into him until she could feel the slick skin of his chest.

"No," he ordered and moved so his penis no longer touched her.

He used his palm to smear liquid soap over her skin, massaging the substance into her muscles, and Sarah arched her spine and pressed against his questing fingers.

The facecloth, now soapy, came into use once more. He stroked her neck and shoulders unhurriedly then moved along her upper spine to her lower back. He glided his hand to her bottom, where he smoothed the toweling material in a circular motion around each buttock. His movements became slower and Sarah squirmed.

Jack pushed her forward and took the cloth lower to wash the backs of her thighs. He parted them and maneuvered the cloth to stroke her cleft. Sarah purred then moaned in desperate need.

She jumped when, minus the facecloth, he trailed his fingers over her wet folds then slipped one finger inside her. She mewled and pressed into his hand.

He plunged a second finger inside her then thrust both in deeper. Sarah bucked her hips. She wanted more from him and she wanted it harder.

Jack obliged. He rubbed her clit with his thumb, his thrusts increasing. Within seconds, Sarah's whole body went rigid as an intense climax shot through her and she cried out when it overtook her.

Jack continued to stroke her relentlessly before he withdrew his fingers and, as if impatient, he entered her quick and hard.

He pulled her backward and she discovered he had crouched a bit so she could almost seat herself on his thighs. He was able to plunge into her even deeper until he filled her.

He thrust into her with strong, measured strokes and slid his palms around to her breasts, cupping and squeezing them.

An electric jolt of excitement rolled through her and Sarah moaned out loud.

He grasped her hips and raised her. He withdrew before he forcefully thrust his way back inside, his pace steady and strong.

He circled her clit with his fingers and pulled her to him, his arm a vise, holding her as his movements increased in pace and power.

The tingle of Sarah's impending second orgasm hit her and she increased her own thrusts to force out the pleasure.

When her orgasm finally took her over — the sensation of exploding, of breaking apart — Jack shouted his own release and came hard inside her. Her sex milked him, her nerves sizzling with overwhelming sensations.

Still inside her, he straightened, causing his cock to slip out of her, and she sank back against him.

Jack licked her earlobe, making her flinch and her legs tremble. She turned in his arms and sighed.

He held her and kissed her neck. His dick hardened again, as if on command, and pressed forcefully to her wet curls — an irresistible temptation.

Jack sighed. "I want you again, but I've got to talk to you. Let's finish in here and go into the bedroom."

Sarah nodded. The 'talk' bit didn't sound good and her spirits sank a little.

Jack went to a closet on the wall, opened the door and took out a large bath towel. He enveloped her in it and dried her, patting the moisture from her hair and skin and caressing each part of her trembling body.

When he'd finished, he saw to himself, slung the towel over a rail and led her from the room.

He made himself comfortable on the bed and leaned against the headboard before he beckoned to her. Sarah went to him, sat beside him with her back to him then half-reclined to rest against his chest. He put his arms around her, his hands clasped under her breasts, and rested his chin on the top of her head.

His warm skin touched her and a lazy sexual desire coiled in her stomach. She ignored it and said, "We always seem to have to talk. What is it, Jack?"

He was silent for a few minutes then rubbed his face on her hair. "It's not good news," he said. "I've got to go back to the ship. There's a problem with some maintenance. Chad has been dealing with it but he needs my help. We'll have to leave first thing tomorrow."

Sarah tensed and her heart plummeted into the pit of her stomach. "I see. So, the bubble bursts."

Jack kissed her neck. "Don't say that, Sarah. You knew our time together had to end at some point."

"I know. I didn't want to think about it and now it's a reality check." Jack stroked her nipple and it immediately hardened and she shivered. "Please, stop," she said breathlessly. "I can't think straight when you do that."

Jack laughed softly. "Sometimes thinking is bad for you."

Sarah squirmed when he continued to caress her breast and familiar feelings coiled between her legs.

She tried to focus on the conversation instead of how his touch was affecting her. "What will happen to…us?"

Jack stopped what he was doing and his muscles tensed. "We'll do our jobs like always, Sarah. We'll have to act normally and it'll be hell. Are you having doubts?"

Sarah rubbed her back on his chest. "Absolutely not," she replied. "I don't know how I'm going to keep my hands off you, though."

When she half-glanced over her shoulder at him, his face was expressionless. Regret filled her when she sensed he'd switched to Navy mode and she'd lost him. His mind was elsewhere, and she couldn't blame him. It was something she understood, but it still left her a little cold, because he'd drifted away from her so fast.

Jack cocked an eyebrow at her questioningly. "Listen... I've gone ahead and booked a room at the Hilton Oceanfront for us when we return from the *BIA*'s shakedown patrol. You'll need to pick up the key card at reception. Use my name. They will be expecting you. We have a two-week furlough when we return. We could stay at the hotel for a night then drive back here. My parents have a log cabin in the woods close by the main house. I thought we might spend our leave there."

Sarah stroked his cheek. Excitement filled her at hearing that he still had plans for them when they returned. She would have him all to herself for fourteen wonderful days.

Jack grinned then kissed her. He licked her lips, flicked her nipple and she jumped.

"As much as I'd love to continue paying attention to your extremely mouthwatering breasts, I think we should get some sleep. We leave at zero seven hundred hours tomorrow."

Sarah made a small moue of disappointment. "If you say so," she said.

Jack laughed and shook her a little. "Are you having a hissy fit?"

Sarah giggled. "No way. I'm trying to think of ways to keep my hands off you when we're onboard ship."

Jack slid down the bed and pulled her with him. "Yeah. It ain't gonna be good. Come on. Let's get some sleep."

Sarah slid down his body, turned away from him and he curved around her, resting his arm across her waist.

In a reflexive response, she pressed her bottom into his groin and ground herself on him. He tapped one of her buttocks.

"Don't go there," he said. "I'm right on the edge of saying 'fuck sleep'."

Sarah's laugh was low but she stopped teasing him and rested her hand atop his, where it nestled on her chest.

She closed her eyes and listened to him breathe, knowing he was still wide awake. She wished they didn't have to leave. She had a premonition that the real world with its restrictions and its hazards to their relationship was going to come rushing back to cause problems. She was filled with foreboding.

Their separation onboard the *BIA* was going to be a test of their self-control and whether their relationship could withstand the rigors of their duties and their obligations to something other than their affair.

It was far from ideal, but Sarah knew her love for him was deep enough that she could handle their enforced separation until they returned to homeport. It was Jack she was concerned about.

He had years of commitment and loyalty to the navy and she sensed that although he hadn't said anything, their entanglement might put him in a position where he'd have to choose between his career and her. Once onboard ship, his feelings could very well be influenced by those very things that made him the man he was. They might well change, to her detriment.

Sarah closed her eyes and relished in Jack's warmth. It was some time before she fell asleep, and when she did, she was restless and full of broken dreams.

Chapter Twenty-Seven

Two days into shakedown patrol

Sarah stepped off the last step of the narrow vertical ladder onto the steel deck of the passageway and hurried toward the Combat Information Center, the CIC. She was now two floors below the bridge and there was a marked difference in the atmosphere, it being far quieter and with an odor that was often present in confined spaces.

Dim red standing lights were installed throughout the interior and lined the bulkheads. They provided enough illumination to permit safe movement of persons within the space when the regular ones were extinguished. Sarah had no problem with them and continued to move quickly toward the CIC.

Her role on the *BIA* was junior officer of the deck, and she assisted the officer of the deck, the OOD. She was in the process of qualifying as a full OOD.

She was due to stand the afternoon watch — noon to sixteen hundred hours — and she was required to report to the CIC at the start of each duty. On her visits there, it was important for her to determine whether any necessary actions were expected to occur during her watch, to check the navigational track, read orders and determine the position of nearby ships.

The CIC was a restricted area where the sensors for launching missiles and heavy ordnance were, and it was the combat heart of the destroyer.

Once Sarah had been given authorization to enter the CIC, she spoke to the senior operations specialist. They went over and clarified any pertinent matters before she left to make her way back to the bridge.

She thought about Jack as she climbed. She hadn't seen him since they'd left homeport forty-eight hours before. She'd known he would have a lot to do in the first few days, with maintenance reports to check, the ship's log to complete and briefings to get through, but she'd hoped she might run into him in the passageways or somewhere away from the rest of the crew.

She couldn't sleep and had no appetite. She knew she was being far from professional and her job might suffer as a result, but her mind repeatedly went over the hours they'd spent together at his parents' home. She couldn't get him out of her head.

She'd been aware from the start that it was going to be difficult but hadn't fully realized how dreadful she would feel and how it would affect her. She reminded herself that he would let her know when he wanted to see her. It would wreck both their careers if she took things into her own hands and attempted to visit him, but it tortured her to know that his quarters were so close and she could do nothing but walk by them.

No matter how many times Sarah went on duty, she never failed to feel awed when she stepped onto the bridge. Apart from the metal staircase on her left, at first glance the area could be mistaken for the modern office of a graphic design firm or, from a fantasy viewpoint, the bridge of the starship from the well-known television series.

Rows of computer stations, each with three glowing monitors with sometimes incomprehensible computer-speak on them, faced toward large screens. They showed the *BIA*'s heading and location in relation to land masses and shoals and any weather systems that might prove a threat to the ship.

Besides the usual keyboards, trackballs and touchscreens, there was a display map showing flight paths and a series of concentric circles representing incoming vessels. More information concerning specific systems appeared on the side monitors.

Outside the ship, lookouts would be placed typically at the stern, near the bow or on or close to the superstructure. Part of the bridge watch's job was to constantly scan the horizon with binoculars as a backup to radar if the equipment missed a small fishing boat or failed to track big waves in a heavy sea. This role was hers.

Sarah approached Master Chief Petty Officer Harris, the quartermaster and a man she knew well because she'd stood many watches with him. She smiled and he nodded a greeting.

She'd also met Lieutenant junior grade Alan Webster, the conning officer, and Lieutenant Mike Simmonds, the JOOD, in the past, and both grinned at her before they returned to their duties.

Sarah approached Lieutenant Webster, stopped in front of him and, as was the custom, said, "I'm ready to relieve you, sir,"

The officer immediately replied, "I'm ready to be relieved, ma'am."

"Anything I should know?" Sarah asked. She listened carefully when the conning officer supplied additional information and reconfirmed what she was already aware of.

When Sarah was fully satisfied that she'd grasped everything, she said, "I relieve you, sir."

The officer responded, "I stand relieved, ma'am. Attention. Lieutenant Morgan has the deck."

Both Sarah and the officer who had been relieved exchanged salutes and Sarah announced, "This is Lieutenant Morgan. I have the deck."

The master chief picked up the ship's log, which he kept close by him, opened it and made an entry to reflect that fact before he signed it.

The new team entered and proceeded with the same procedure for relieving their counterparts, and Sarah walked to the windows to take up her post. She nodded at the XO when she caught his eye.

She thought she detected a quizzical expression on his face as he stared at her and wondered if there was a problem. He was silent, however, and she shrugged mentally and turned to stare out of the window.

The captain's chair with the XO's alongside it was approximately a foot from her. She checked it out of the corner of her eye and anticipation swarmed in her stomach. Jack would be joining the team soon and she would see him for the first time since they'd returned to the destroyer.

The next four hours were going to be extremely difficult, and it would be a tough test for them both. They would be in a confined space with one another, and while they were professionals—he more so than she—their secret relationship was going to place them both under a lot of strain. There was no doubt they had to get through it if their affair was going to continue.

Sarah picked up heavy compass binoculars but she paused a moment before she brought them to her eyes and stared at the scene in front of her.

She estimated the *BIA* was doing fifteen knots, which was half-ahead, and the ship was cruising smoothly in light seas. Sarah had checked the weather report and knew there was a gentle breeze of ten knots with large wavelets of approximately two-to-four feet, with crests beginning to break and scattered whitecaps.

The destroyer's bow plunged into the troughs between the waves, and cream-colored foam and spray soared skyward and spilled over the ship's railing to fleck her deck.

The horizon stretched for Sarah's entire field of view in the most spectacular fashion, with the sky an infinite pale blue canopy dominated by the sun, which resembled a blazing fireball whose rays glittered on the deep blue water.

Two seagulls circled in the air, one diving toward the surface of the sea only to rise again, the other riding the currents in a dance of freedom.

Sarah watched the hovering bird for a few minutes and raised the binoculars to her eyes. She scanned a one-hundred-and-eighty-degree arc from port to starboard, alert for any obstacles or another vessel posing an imminent threat.

She was not so engrossed in her task that she failed to hear, above the quiet conversation of the team, heavy footsteps ringing on the ladder. She recognized who it was even before he appeared.

"Captain on the bridge," the master chief called out and Sarah about-turned and stood to attention.

She stared ahead — as was expected — but Jack was directly in her field of vision. When he approached, her face flushed and she bit her lip, trying hard to avoid looking at him.

He was staring at her, however, his usual impassive expression present. As he drew close and the rest of the team was behind him, he winked at her and the corner of his mouth lifted.

He turned to Chad Mason and they spoke for a few minutes before the XO made his way across the deck and disappeared down the ladder. His footsteps faded as he descended to the lower levels of the ship.

Sarah's heart lurched and she swallowed when Jack turned to face her. His arm brushed hers as he passed her on his way to his chair and she heard him say in a low voice, "Sorry about that, Lieutenant."

Sarah cleared her throat. "No problem, sir," she said, and wondered if her voice sounded as husky as she thought it did.

Jack sat and, once he was comfortable said, "Helmsman, I have the deck and the conn."

The OOD, who was the recipient of orders and who relayed them to whoever it was meant for, echoed, "Aye, aye, sir. Helmsman, the captain has the deck and the conn."

The Helmsman reiterated the order for the third time. "Aye, sir. The captain has the deck and the conn."

"Very well," the conning officer said, confirming that the order had been fully noted.

"Steady as she goes, Helmsman," Jack continued.

The conning officer responded, "Aye, aye, sir. Helmsman, steady as she goes."

The Helmsman confirmed the order, "Aye, sir. Steady as she goes."

"Very well."

Sarah turned to face front and, as she did, the ship's bell rang twice to signal that an hour of the watch had passed.

Sarah peeked furtively at Jack and her stomach fluttered at how good he looked in his working service uniform. He noticed her staring at him and his mouth twitched, as if he were about to smile.

"Everything okay, Lieutenant?" he asked.

Sarah raised the binoculars to her eyes once more and answered equally quietly, "As good as it can be, sir."

She scanned the horizon once more, but her mind was on the man next to her. He was so close that she could reach out and touch him. It was all she wanted to do and it took every ounce of control to stop herself from throwing herself into his arms. There was nothing for her to do but suck it up.

"I'll see you later," he said, his tone pitched even lower.

Sarah swallowed and tried to maintain her composure at his words. "Yes, sir."

Chapter Twenty-Eight

It was a constant battle for Sarah not to turn her head in Jack's direction. She carried out her duties meticulously and with as much concentration as she could muster, but all the while she sensed him there beside her.

Occasionally he would speak to her regarding a report, headings or data confirmation. She answered him in as steady a voice as possible, but she wanted to lean in to him, and as the hours went by, it became harder and harder to maintain a cool, calm exterior.

At fifteen fifty-five hours, Jack gave the deck and the conn back to the conning officer and rose to leave. He passed the master chief and as he did so, Sarah heard him order, "I'm going to my quarters, Master Chief. Can you get Lieutenant Morgan to report to me with the ship's log once her watch is over?"

"Yes, sir," the master chief replied. He stared at Sarah and cocked a questioning eyebrow at her.

Sarah shrugged, because Jack's order was an excuse and a pointless request. He had access to the log on his computer, but as an order from the captain was one to be obeyed regardless of how odd it sounded, it had to be carried out without question.

Shortly thereafter, eight bells struck and the relief watch entered the bridge to relieve Sarah's team.

Once her counterpart had taken over, she was handed the log and she left in a hurry. Her heart raced at breakneck speed and elation surged through her. She wanted to get to him, and she nearly fell down the ladders in her haste and jogged along the passageway toward officer country.

Sarah was nearing Jack's door when Mike Stevens called her name from behind her. It would have appeared strange if she'd ignored him, so she stopped and waited for him to join her, tapping the toe of her boot impatiently.

"Hey, gorgeous," Mike said, his voice overly loud in the narrow confines of the corridor.

Sarah forced herself to smile. "What's wrong?" she asked.

"I haven't seen you around lately. Where've you been?"

"I've been doing my job. Listen, the captain wants to see me."

Mike touched her wrist and stroked it. "Stay a bit."

"Mike, I—"

Sarah froze when she heard a door open behind her. She winced inwardly when Jack said, "I thought I'd asked to see you, Lieutenant."

She glared at Mike, who mouthed, "Sorry," before he about-faced and went back the way he'd come.

Sarah faced Jack, who said in a cold voice, "In here."

At the look on his face, she went to him. He stepped aside to let her enter, after which he slammed the door shut behind her.

He stood close to her so she could see that the blue of his eyes had become dark and turbulent—a warning sign he was angry—and a muscle flickered in his jaw.

"The log, sir," she said and handed it to him.

Jack snatched it from her and tossed it over his shoulder. "Screw the log."

Sarah watched it land on the floor before she focused on his face.

He folded his arms. "What was that about?"

Sarah understood now why he was angry. "With M— Lieutenant Stevens? It was nothing."

"No? That little scene didn't look like nothing. He looked like he was being a bit too friendly. Was he?"

Sarah shook her head. "Mike's always been like that. He's an outrageous flirt."

Jack shook his head. "I don't like the way he acts with you."

"He wasn't hitting on me specifically, Jack. He does it with all women."

"Yeah, well... Okay, but this is new territory for me and I don't like it."

Sarah touched his arm. She could feel the tension in his muscles and she stroked the material of his jacket to calm him. "Jack, you don't have to be jealous. I only care about you."

Jack looked at his boots then stared into her face, his eyes probing and intense.

"I've missed you," Sarah said. "The last two days have been hell."

"Yeah? Tell me about it," Jack said and unfolded his arms.

He took a single pace toward her and pulled her roughly to him. He guided her backward and pinned her to the door.

He covered her mouth in a hard and urgent kiss. She whimpered with discomfort before she opened her mouth and let his tongue entwine with hers. She pulled his head down and trailed her fingers from his neck down to his chest. She moved to his stomach then to his groin, where she pressed her palm against his stiff cock.

Jack groaned and skimmed one hand from her waist to the front of her fatigue trousers. He roughly parted her legs and stroked her folds through the thick material.

Sarah was instantly and gloriously wet from his touch. She moaned and pushed onto his fingers, and he rubbed and circled her clit hard.

She could feel the stillness and the tingling sensation which preceded her orgasm, and she quickly undid the fastening of his pants and unzipped him. She plunged her fingers inside his shorts and grasped him.

Jack groaned and undid her trousers. He pushed his hand into her panties and began to stimulate her clit for real. He thrust two fingers deep inside her and Sarah's climax coiled and built.

"Jack," she murmured, "*please.*"

She pumped his cock hard and heard him groan again. His penis throbbed and she only managed to do a few more strokes before he buried his face in her shoulder. She heard him utter a muffled shout and he came, his hot juice spurting over her hand.

Sarah's orgasm exploded inside her at the same time and she buried her scream in his jacket. She quaked and shook with pleasure and clung to him, because if she'd let go, she would have fallen to the floor.

Jack withdrew his fingers and clasped her waist to hold her up. Her body trembled and he kissed her mouth then reached toward his desk and grabbed some tissues that were in a box.

He pulled one out and handed it to her. "Here."

Sarah took what was offered and wiped her hands. She balled the material and shoved it into her jacket pocket, then she rested her forehead against his jacket.

"Hey. Are you okay?" Jack asked.

Sarah shook her head. "No," she said her voice muffled by his chest. "Nothing's okay."

"Shh-h," Jack said. He rubbed her back in a soothing circular motion. "I'm sorry. That wasn't meant to happen. I didn't get you in here for that."

Sarah raised her eyes to his and smiled at the sheepish and concerned look on his face.

"You don't have to apologize. We both came unglued."

"I've wanted you so damn bad. It's tearing me apart being away from you."

"I know. But we have got to do it this way, Jack. We've only got five more days, then we can be together."

"Sure," Jack said, but even though he agreed with her, Sarah thought he sounded unsure.

"I should go," she said. "Someone might catch us."

"I guess you're right."

Jack cupped Sarah's chin with a warm hand and kissed her on the lips. When he stepped back from her, he said, "I'll see you — and keep away from Lieutenant Stevens."

Sarah traced the outline of his lips with her finger. "You *are* jealous."

He tensed. "Yeah. Now you know. I don't think I'm a nice guy when I get like that."

"There're no need for you to be. You're the only man I care about." She kissed him and ran the tip of her tongue along his bottom lip. "I've got to get going."

Jack let her go and Sarah fastened her pants. Before she left, she looked over her shoulder at him. "See you later," she whispered and watched him nod, his gaze still locked with hers.

Sarah opened the door, stepped out into the passageway and closed it. She turned to hurry toward her own room and almost cannoned into the XO, who stood in front of her, his eyebrows raised questioningly.

She stepped backward and uneasiness dispelled the sexual excitement which still swarmed through her body. She pressed herself to the bulkhead so he could get past her.

"Sir," she said politely.

Commander Mason walked past her, his gaze still on her face. He nodded at her and said, "Lieutenant," and as soon as he was behind her, Sarah swallowed and ran to her room.

Chapter Twenty-Nine

Twenty-four hours had passed since the unplanned passionate meeting with Sarah in his quarters, and Jack was on the bridge. He stared through the binoculars at the distant horizon but struggled to focus on what he was doing. His mind was distracted, his thoughts elsewhere.

There was nothing for him to do and he was restless. They'd reached the coordinates for their shakedown patrol and begun maneuvers to check equipment, which included target practice with the deck gun. He was beyond pleased that the *BIA* had performed well when she'd been put her through her paces.

In forty-eight hours, he would turn her toward homeport. In four days, he would say a temporary goodbye to her and be with Sarah. For now, the destroyer was on a new heading and proceeding full ahead into a sapphire-colored ocean to monitor the performance of her engines.

The sky was a deep cloudless blue, the sea running calm, with wavelets topped with white foam parting on each side of the warship to form a churning wake astern. The ship's bow cleaved the water and spume sprayed into the air, sparkling in the bright sunlight like diamonds tossed onto a turquoise canvas.

Jack heard murmured voices from the team on watch but didn't pay attention to them, which was a first. The only thing on his mind was Sarah, how young she was and how like a jealous old man *he* was. It irritated him.

His jealousy was groundless, because she'd done nothing to make him mistrust her—however, he couldn't bear the idea of other men showing an interest in her. He wasn't in the least surprised that they hovered about her like bees near honey, and he hated the feelings of vulnerability and insecurity when he thought about it.

Off ship he might be able to do something, *if* he wanted to risk letting their relationship become common knowledge. Onboard, his hands were tied in relation to the lengths he could go to warn off other admirers. He felt frustrated and threatened, emotions which didn't sit well with him. He was not in a good place in his head.

Jack shifted in his chair, uncomfortable with his thoughts. He was determined to concentrate on his job and he focused intently on the horizon and the hazy demarcation between sea and sky.

He'd taken over his JOOD's task of keeping watch when the young officer had been summoned to look over some weather system data, and he vowed he would forget about Sarah for the time being.

He saw a sudden movement on the foc'sle and swung the binoculars to see who or what it was. He saw Sarah saunter to the rail with its interconnecting mesh chain link barrier. When she reached it, she leaned on in it and posed as if she were studying the water. His heart pounded hard.

She remained in the position for a few moments then turned, rested both elbows on the metal rail and stared up at the bridge, straight into his eyes.

Jack kept his gaze on her. He stared at her breasts which, by her position, were pushed toward him in a provocative manner, her uniform jacket straining and molding the full mounds.

Through the powerful lenses, he watched her lick her lips and smile seductively before she subtly thrust her hips forward.

Jack grinned to himself, although his body tensed and his cock hardened.

You little tease.

His sexual arousal intensified as she pushed her shoulders farther back and arched her spine so it looked as though she was offering herself to him. He would have taken her if he could, because now his hard-on was a bulging prominence in the front of his pants.

She suddenly straightened and a moment later a man joined her. With a twist of Jack's gut, he recognized Lieutenant Stevens. As soon as he neared her, Sarah smiled and glanced quickly up at the bridge.

"Damn," he muttered. "Fuck this shit."

He almost slammed the binoculars down beside him. Once more, jealousy ate at him. He turned his gaze away from Sarah and the young officer and gritted his teeth together with anger and resentment. His feelings were not only childish but unreasonable, and he couldn't rid himself of the thought that he was acting irrationally.

Okay. So, they're talking. She's entitled to talk to whomever she wants. I don't own her, we're not married and you're being an asshole, Jack Chalmers. But I fucking hate it.

Jack sighed and rested his foot on the wide shelf that ran around the bridge on three sides.

He stared glumly out of the windows and wondered what in the hell he was going to do about the mess he found himself in.

* * * *

Sarah made her way along the dimly lit passageway toward her room. She'd finished the middle watch, which had been from midnight to zero four hundred hours, and she was exhausted. All she wanted now was to get to her bunk and sleep eight hours straight until her next duty.

She was even too tired to think about Jack. Her eyelids drooped and she yawned, her jaw cracking. She was in desperate need of sleep.

She was almost dozing on her feet when she passed the heads, and she jumped with shock when her right arm was grabbed and she was yanked into the gloomy interior.

Jack had been waiting for her, and before she could utter a protest, he'd pulled her to a shower stall at the far end of the room and pushed her inside.

She stood uncertainly as he closed and locked the door. He stepped two paces to stand in front of her and placed a hand on either side of her head. He rested his palms on the steel partition of the shower cubicle and lowered his face until his mouth was inches from her own.

"Jack," Sarah whispered. "What the hell are you doing?"

"I needed to see you," he answered.

Sarah smiled, elation surging through her at his admission that he was desperate to be with her. Her tiredness vanished, but as much as she wanted to fall into his arms, worry regarding the risk he was taking and which involved her, forced her to restrain herself.

"I want to be with you too, but, Jack, someone could catch us."

Jack's eyes were stormy and he shrugged. "I don't give a damn, Sarah. It's driving me nuts. Fuck knows what's come over me, but I can't stay away from you. I didn't know this was going to be so hard."

Jack's mouth covered hers and she winced at his urgent kiss, because he bruised her lips.

She clutched the front of his jacket and pulled him close. As she did, he took his hands from the metal wall and grasped her hips, pulling her so she was pressed to his groin.

He drew back from her mouth and murmured, "Do you feel me?"

He was all rigid, hot cock through his pants, and she slid her hips first one way then the other.

"Yes," Sarah murmured. "And I want you inside me and I want you to make love to me."

Jack slammed his mouth on hers and she had to force herself not to moan when his lips seared her.

Pleasurable sensations built in her stomach and burned her cleft, and she skimmed her palms down his spine to his bottom and pulled him to her – hard.

Jack pushed her against the steel wall, and by the expression on his face and the tension in his body, he was hungry for her and didn't care what risks he took.

As much as Sarah was desperate for him, she couldn't let him be discovered acting like a rampant teenager getting a quick feel in a public restroom. She pushed at his chest and dragged her mouth away from his.

"Jack," she whispered, "we should stop."

At first, she thought he hadn't heard her, and she cupped his face between her hands.

His breathing was harsh and he stared at her as if she was someone he didn't know.

"What?" he asked at last.

"We have to go before someone catches us."

Jack was silent then he made a small sound of defeat. "Yeah. I'm sorry."

Sarah placed a chaste kiss on his mouth. "Hey," she said. "You keep apologizing. I would do anything to be with you, but we can't. It's too risky."

As if to confirm her fears, she heard footsteps ring in the passageway outside the heads. She froze and held her breath, and Jack's body stiffened.

The unknown person carried on past and Sarah slumped against the wall. Jack groaned. "Holy shit," he muttered, "that was close."

He unlocked the shower door and they crossed the floor as quietly as their boots would allow. They reached the exit and Jack kissed her on her mouth. "I'll see you later," he said, and winked at her.

Sarah touched his face and left him, hurrying along the passageway toward officer country.

She was relieved they hadn't been discovered, but her emotions were in crisis when she remembered the demanding way in which he'd caressed her body.

There were three days of patrol left and it was going to take all her self-control to stop herself from going to his quarters and dissolving into his arms. Their relationship depended on her showing restraint.

Chapter Thirty

Jack closed the door to his quarters, barely stopping himself from slamming it behind him. He walked to the middle of the floor and put his fisted hands on his hips.

He was still breathing heavily from his brief but potent encounter with Sarah, and for a second he felt as if his own self was slipping away.

Where the fuck is your head, buddy? You need to sort yourself out.

Jack loved Sarah more than life itself. The impossible situation he found himself in, however—all based on his inability to avoid her—was culminating in a trap that he was becoming enmeshed in more deeply every minute he spent in her company and which he knew was about to snap shut.

His reckless behavior was going to get them both caught because his self-control was unraveling, and he was on his way to losing everything.

If he wanted to hold on to what he had, he needed to sort out the situation one way or the other. He had no idea what the solution was, but the idea that he was even thinking along those lines knotted his gut and filled him with a feeling of loss.

He shook his head and went to a coffee machine on a bookcase. He poured himself a cup of the dark liquid and was about to take a sip when there was a knock on the door.

"Yeah. It's open," Jack said and Chad Morris poked his head round it. Jack frowned at the unexpected appearance of his XO. "Hey. What's up? Problem?"

Chad shook his head. "Nope. Everything is green. Have you got a few minutes though?"

Jack went to his desk and sat on its corner. He sipped his beverage and answered, "Sure. Come on in. Help yourself to coffee, if you want some."

Chad stepped into the room and closed the door behind him. He shook his head. "I'm good, thanks."

Jack watched his friend walk toward and stop in front of him. He stared at his XO's face and had an idea he was going to have to listen to something he might not want to hear.

Chad folded his arms. "Listen, Jack," he said. "We've been good buddies for a helluva long time. Or at least, I like to think we have been."

"We have. Something on your mind?" Jack said.

Chad hesitated then said, "Shit. There's no easy way to do this, so I'm gonna go right ahead and ask it. Is there anything going on between you and Lieutenant Morgan?"

Jack's body tensed and his heart lurched in his chest. *Oh, fuck. He knows.*

"I don't know what you're getting at," he said in a casual voice.

"Holy shit, Jack. Don't give me that. I was walking past here the other night and she came haring out of here like a bat out of hell. She was like a rabbit caught in headlights, and excuse me for being blunt, but she looked like she'd been screwed."

Jack grimaced, and a stab of annoyance at the way his XO was talking about Sarah pierced his gut.

He drew in a deep breath. "It's none of your goddamn business," he said.

Chad sighed. "I was hoping you might come clean, Jack. It *is* my business. If there's something going on between you and her, then *you* know that if someone finds out, you're both going to be up to your necks in shit. It'll fuck up both of your careers. So stop bullshitting me."

Chad's face wore a serious expression and Jack was positive he would see through any excuses he came up with.

"Shit. Okay. Yeah, there is something going on," he admitted at last.

Chad uncrossed his arms. "Jesus fuck, Jack. What the hell are you thinking?" He was silent for a moment. "You know the rules. You enforce 'em, for fuck's sake."

Jack stood and paced the floor, running his hand in agitation through his hair. "Don't you think I know that?" he said.

"You do know that if you're caught it would end in an inquiry, and if you're found guilty, the result will be dismissal, forfeiture of pay and-or confinement for two years. Throw in a charge of sexual misconduct as well and they'll throw the book at you, pal. You're a senior captain, Jack. What's gotten into you?"

Anger stirred in Jack but he stayed silent, because he had no defense against his friend's harsh words.

Chad stared at him. "Is the relationship serious?"

Jack hated having to answer the questions being thrown at him. He did love Sarah, but it was personal and he didn't want to discuss it like it was some sort of 'wham, bam, thank you, ma'am' affair. But Chad had him pinned and he couldn't avoid replying with anything but the truth.

"Yeah. It's serious," he replied. "Dead serious."

Chad sighed. "I can see that, buddy. It's written all over your face. I'm sorry, but you should think good and hard where this is going. And it's not just you. It's Lieutenant Morgan as well. You might get off with nothing more than a kick up the ass. She won't."

"So...your point is?" Jack asked, his tone hard and cold. "I'm supposed to say 'sorry, Sarah, it's over. I might get shit-canned, so see ya'?"

Chad shook his head and the sympathetic expression on his face was sincere. "I can't tell you what to do, buddy. We've known each other for a long time, so I'm not here as your XO but as someone who knows you, Jack. You need to sort this out before the shit hits the fan. I'm being serious here."

"Okay. Talking as friends, Chad, I'm in fucking hell. I knew what would happen to both me and her if it carried on and that I was gonna lose her at some point. You think I didn't know what it might lead to from the beginning? Sarah said something to me about living in a bubble and when it burst, that's when everything would bite us in the ass. She was right." Jack slammed his mug on his desk. "Goddammit. God-fucking-dammit all to hell."

Chad was silent for a second before he said, "As I said, I can't tell you how to handle the situation. But, if I noticed something is going on, so will the rest of the crew. And if it leaks out to the brass, it's *finito* for the both of you."

An icy knot formed in Jack's stomach. There was a pain in his chest, as though his heart was being ripped apart. He was torn. Sarah or their careers? She was young, and if they broke up, she could move on, find another man her own age, and eventually she would forget about him.

He was horrified with the direction his thoughts were going. He was considering letting her go, but he loved her, so how could he be thinking along those lines? Was his commitment to his profession more important than her? If he was thinking that way, he must have doubts about continuing their affair.

Jack gritted his teeth. "Holy fucking shit. Okay. I'll deal with it. I can't say I appreciate you reminding me of my duty, but I respect you for doing it as my friend. I'll think on it, but I'll get it sorted, one way or the other," he said.

"I really am sorry, Jack." Chad looked at his watch. "Anyway, I need some shut-eye."

"Yeah," Jack answered, his thoughts already moving on to the serious thinking he was going to have to do and the shit choice he would have to make.

Chad turned, went to the door and opened it. He left, closing it quietly behind him.

Jack pulled his chair out and sat in it. He rubbed his hands tiredly over his face and stared at the wood grain of his desk.

"Fuck no," he murmured and closed his eyes.

Chapter Thirty-One

The steel bulkheads of the passageway gleamed dully in the dim light as Sarah made her way toward her room. She'd finished first watch — from twenty hundred hours to midnight — and was desperate for some rack time.

The opportunity to relax and sleep was a moot point. She was due back on duty in the morning at zero four hundred hours and was required to be on the bridge well in advance of the handover, particularly as there was a storm system bearing down on them.

Since she and Jack had been back onboard the *BIA*, her downtime had been eaten away by her thoughts of him. She missed everything about him, and when she did try to get some rest, the memories of their being together resulted in her tossing and turning until she rose early, tired and stressed out.

Sarah felt worse now than she'd done in the past few days. She hadn't seen Jack, even though he took the conn at least twice a day. The last time she'd met with him was when he'd waylaid her to take her into the head.

It concerned her, because it wasn't like him, and with the storm on its way, she would have expected him to be at his post to check that procedures for heavy weather were adhered to and to sign off on such orders.

She'd nearly reached Jack's quarters and her pace slowed as she mulled over the idea of seeing if he was awake. As much as she was desperate for that, it would be irresponsible and stupid. She would be taking a serious risk if she visited him without being summoned, particularly as the crew would shortly be up and about.

Her heart ached, but Sarah walked past his rooms, determined not to glance at the brass nameplate on his door.

She was startled when it opened and Jack said quietly, "Lieutenant, I need a word."

She immediately sensed something was wrong. He was still dressed in his working uniform and his voice was cold. When she turned to face him, the inscrutable look was back on his face and her heart plummeted to rest in the lower regions of her stomach.

"Yes, sir," she said.

When he stepped aside to let her in, her legs shook as she crossed the threshold.

Once inside the room, Sarah stopped and Jack closed the door behind her. Her agitation increased when, instead of kissing her as he always did, he moved away from her, leaned on the corner of his desk, folded his arms, crossed his ankles and stared at the floor.

Unsure if this was a personal or formal summons, Sarah stood at attention, her eyes on him, waiting.

The silence stretched between them, and at last he looked at her and cleared his throat.

Sarah noticed a look of anguish on his face and nausea churned in her stomach. She knew why she was there and what the outcome was going to be.

She wanted to stop him from speaking the first word, to plead with him to reconsider and convince him their relationship could continue despite the hazards and obstacles in their way. As if he sensed she was going to try to sway him, Jack shook his head.

"Don't, Sarah. I'm sorry. We can't go on. It has to end," he said, and his tone sounded flat and emotionless.

His words pierced the silence like icy shards and the floor rocked. Sarah felt weightless, as if the hard surface had dropped from underneath her.

She tried to speak, couldn't and swallowed. At last she managed to regain her voice and said, "I don't understand—"

Jack uncrossed his ankles with something like agitation. "It's not your fault, Sarah. It's mine. I should never have let anything happen between us. It goes against everything I believe in to have let it get so out of control."

Sarah shook her head mutely, both in denial and in opposition to him laying the blame at his own door. She tried to stop the shaking which had overtaken her, but her body denied her even that.

"I thought…we had something," she said.

Jack ran a hand through his hair and folded his arms once more. "We did… We do. But it's not enough. I feel so goddamn guilty that I might ruin your career. You've a lot to offer, Sarah, and you could succeed in whatever you do. And there's also mine to consider and I don't think I'm prepared to give it up for anyone."

His harsh statement shook her and she wanted to scream. For him to tell her it had been a waste of time and their relationship wasn't worth any further trouble filled her with an emotion so desolate that she wanted to kick up a storm like a child.

It was obvious she'd meant nothing to him. She should have known it would end on this note. An affair between a high-ranking officer and a lieutenant was a no-go right from the start.

There were too many drawbacks and hurdles, but in her love for him and in desperate hope there'd been a chance for them, she'd lived in denial...as had he.

Sarah bit her lip until she tasted the salty tang of blood. She wasn't going to let him see her cry, so she straightened her spine even more and raised her chin with determination.

"You're a bastard," she said. Anger stirred in her and she welcomed it. "You were telling the truth when you quoted the rule book to me. I should have listened to you. Instead, I acted like a whore and threw myself at you. I should never have let myself get involved with you. It was stupid of me to ever think you cared enough for me to fight for us."

"Sarah—"

At the use of her name, Sarah held up her hand to silence him. "It's Lieutenant, *Captain*," she said, forcing her voice to sound uncaring and hard. "Do me a favor. From now on, we'll only meet on the bridge, so don't speak to me unless it's in the line of duty. Stay away from me."

She choked on her words and had to stop speaking.

Jack stared at her in silence, the expression on his face as hard as she'd ever seen it.

Sarah hadn't finished, "You won't have to worry that I'll let the cat out of the bag and get you into trouble either. It's not worth talking about. As you said, it's finished."

The brief anger had dissipated and a scream of anguish began to build inside her. She had to get out of his quarters, because the look on his face was breaking her heart.

"Am I dismissed, sir?" she asked and stared at the dark wood paneling behind him.

"You're dismissed, Morgan," he said.

Sarah faced the door and gripped the knob. She turned it violently but it slipped from her grasp. She held her breath, grabbed it once more and wrenched it open so hard that it slammed against the bulkhead with a resounding crash.

She left in double-time, leaving it open. Her eyes flooded with hot tears, which she struggled to keep back. She prayed she wouldn't meet anyone in the passageways, as her heartbreak would be on display for everyone to see.

She ran to the room she shared with Babs. It was empty when she arrived, her friend on duty in the CIC, and she let herself in. A single security light created shadows in the corners of the narrow room, with its basic bunk beds and a couple of functional lockers. The air was redolent with the scent of two women sharing — perfume and deodorant — but the comforting odors did nothing to ease Sarah's distraught frame of mind.

She sat on the bottom bunk and wondered how she could feel so much pain and not break apart. She thought of the words Jack had said to her and covered her face with her hands.

Disbelief, torment and confusion tore at her mind and she groaned. Her world had been turned upside down and she wanted to huddle under her blankets, fall asleep and never wake up.

Sarah swung her legs onto the bunk, lay on her side and curled into a fetal position. Her heart thundered in her chest and she wanted and needed to cry, because the breakdown might have gone some way to relieving the tearing torment inside her. She remained numb and empty, the tears locked in her throat, her heartbreak unbearable.

Chapter Thirty-Two

Sarah hadn't slept since she'd left Jack's quarters, and she was exhausted. She wished she could feel angry at his duplicity and the way he'd led her on then dumped her, but she didn't even have that satisfaction.

Shock coursed through her system, and no matter how often she searched her mind to find a reason as to why things had gone so wrong between them, she failed to find a suitable explanation except that he'd never cared for her as much as she did him.

Sarah had dozed on and off, waking numerous times to a dark, empty room and to a sense of unhappiness and loss that gnawed at her and grew in intensity until it was a physical pain.

Eventually, she'd realized it was useless to try to sleep. Her mind wouldn't let her. She rose, tidied her hair, straightened her uniform and left her room to make her way to the mess deck.

Once there, she made herself a mug of coffee and sat at a table in a corner of the room. A half-dozen crew members — either coming off or going on duty — were scattered around the large room consuming early breakfasts or drinking juice or hot beverages. A radio played low in the background, intermixed with murmured conversation and the hum of air conditioning.

Steam curled from the hot liquid and she clasped the thick china in her cold hands, the warmth bringing some relief to her chilled body.

There were no words to describe how she was feeling and it was pointless to try. She needed to sift through her chaotic emotions and work out how she was going to handle her immediate future aboard the *BIA*.

Time was a luxury she didn't have, though, and she would have to bury her emotions and avoid Jack Chalmers like the plague until they homeported, where she could escape to lick her wounds.

"Hey, girl, how've you been?"

The female voice startled Sarah and her hand jerked. Hot coffee spilled onto her fingers and she hissed with pain, set the mug on the table then shook her hand to ease the discomfort.

She glanced up and saw it was Babs. She forced a smile onto her numb lips and tried to make her tone as light as possible, "Hey, long time, no see." Their duties had caused them to be on opposite schedules.

As close as she was to her friend and bunkmate, she didn't intend to let her know about her heartache. It would mean she would have to volunteer information about her disastrous short-lived relationship with their commanding officer. She was bound not to, not just for her sake but his as well.

Babs looked at Sarah with a quizzical expression on her pretty face. "Yeah. Let me go grab a coffee and we'll catch up. I've just come off duty and I'm parched," she said.

Sarah's heart sank. She sensed Babs knew something was wrong and wasn't going to let it go. Her friend knew her too well and she watched as she left to get her drink. She sipped her own, wondering how she was going to explain herself.

A few moments later, Babs arrived back, dragged a chair out and sat. She settled in her seat, stretched out her legs and sighed.

She placed her mug on the table and studied Sarah, her gaze critical. "You look like shit, hon," she announced.

Sarah stared at her hands and nodded. "I couldn't sleep, which is why I'm here haunting the mess decks. I'm on watch in a few hours because of the storm."

Her tone sounded false, even to her own ears, and she was in no doubt that Babs would notice.

The other woman was silent for a moment, then leaned forward so she was close to Sarah. "I saw…something the other night as I was coming off duty and going to our room," she said and glanced over her shoulder to make sure nobody was close enough to overhear her.

Sarah managed to smile. "A ghost?" she asked.

Babs didn't return her smile, which set alarm bells ringing in Sarah's head.

"No ghost. I caught sight of…Captain Chalmers, our illustrious commanding officer, man-handling a certain lieutenant into the head."

Sarah's heart beat faster. She stared into Babs' green eyes, noting that her friend was fully aware of who the lieutenant was.

Feigning nonchalance, Sarah shrugged. "Did you?"

"Yeah. It was goddamn clear that they were really into each other. They didn't even notice I was there."

Sarah bit her lip and shifted nervously in her chair.

Babs was persistent. "Sarah?"

"What do you want me to say, Babs?"

Her voice had lowered even further when Babs said, "I want you to tell me why you were sneaking into the showers with our CO. That clinch was so hot that I'm surprised the damn ship didn't care fire."

Sarah cleared her throat. "Don't ask me about it. I can't tell you."

"Okay... If it had been someone else who'd seen you, do you think you'd be sitting talking to me now? You'd both be shit-canned, Sarah."

Sarah rubbed her forehead. When she spoke, for the first time since she'd left her room, tears filled her eyes, "Do you think I don't know that?"

Babs touched Sarah's hand where it lay on the table. "Sarah! What *have* you done?"

Sarah sighed. "You wouldn't believe me if I told you."

"Try me."

Sarah glanced around to see if anyone was paying attention to their conversation. She confirmed that they were being ignored then she brushed her fingers along her forehead again. She stared intently at her friend. "You have to promise me that what I say will stay between us."

"You have my word."

Sarah shook her head. "I need more than that, Babs. If what I tell you gets out, it could destroy...Captain Chalmers, and I can't have that. You have to swear you'll keep quiet."

Babs frowned and looked annoyed. "Sarah, I would *never* break a confidence."

Sarah studied the other woman's face, watching her expression to see if there was any insincerity in it. There was only honesty and concern, and she sighed again and drew in a deep breath. Exhaling, she said, "Okay. Remember the night of the ball, when I said I was going to take a walk on the beach?"

Babs nodded, staying silent.

"I was attacked."

Babs gasped and went to speak but Sarah held up a hand to stop her. "Let me finish. You *were* right. It was stupid of me to go walking by myself. A homeless guy assaulted me and Jack...Captain Chalmers got him off me and sent him packing. He nearly killed him.

"I've been attracted to Jack for ages, ever since I first came onboard the *BIA*. Futile and pathetic, I know, but we can't help who we fall for, right? The dance he and I had? I thought...there was something there then, but as you so rightly commented, he was my CO and I honestly didn't entertain the idea that something could happen between us.

"It *did* happen, though. He was injured in the fight with the guy who attacked me and I took him back to my room to treat a cut he had on his head. I'm not going to go into details about what happened that night, but the next day he invited me to his family home to attend his sister's wedding. We've been together until last night, when he told me it was over."

Sarah choked on the words and stopped speaking. Silence stretched between them then Babs shook her head, an expression of disbelief on her face.

"Holy shit, Sarah. What the fuck?"

"Yeah, that sounds about right," Sarah responded. She blinked away the tears which filled her eyes.

"I can't believe you both risked your *fucking* jobs for a romp in the hay," Babs said.

Sarah stiffened. "You're wrong," she snapped, her tone cold. "It wasn't a quick fling, not on my part or his. The feelings were there during the six months in the Mediterranean. We didn't know how the other felt, but they were mutual. We all know the regulations about fraternization among the crew and the trouble it can cause."

Her voice shook when she continued, "It got way out of control. He couldn't handle it. You know how he is and I respect his decision—but it doesn't help."

Babs stared at Sarah with an expression of sympathy on her face. "I'm so sorry, Sarah. Do you love him?"

Sarah clenched her friend's hand. "Yes, I do. Pathetic, isn't it?"

Babs shook her head. "No, it's not, babe. But you sure picked the wrong guy." She paused. "What reason did he give you for saying it was over?"

"He felt guilty. If it leaked that we were having a relationship, it might have destroyed his career and would definitely ruin mine."

"That was noble of him."

"No. He did try to convince me we shouldn't get involved, but I managed to...persuade him we could deal with any complications that cropped up. I was wrong."

"Oh, honey, that's one helluva mess. Can't it be worked out?"

Misery knotted Sarah's stomach. "When we get to homeport, I'm getting out of here. I need to clear my head. I can't think straight when I'm near him."

Babs squeezed her hand. "I'm going to my parents'. Do you want to come with?"

Sarah shook her head. "Thanks, Babs, but I want to be on my own. I wouldn't be good company, I'm afraid."

"Okay. But you have my cell phone number if you need me for anything."

Sarah managed a smile. "You got it," she replied and looked at her watch. "I've got to go. Thanks for listening and being such a great friend."

She stood and picked up her mug.

Babs touched her arm. "Sarah? Remember... When we get back to homeport, call me if you need me, okay?"

Sarah's bottom lip trembled. Before she broke down, she nodded and left to wash her cup in the sink, dry it and set it with the others.

She left the mess and went along the passageway toward the ladder that descended into the bowels of the ship to the CIC. She still had some time to spare, but she wanted to report for duty and be at her post well in advance of Jack arriving.

Being among the crew and with bad weather on its way would give her the opportunity to stay busy and keep her distracted. She might even be able to ignore him.

She received authorization to enter the CIC and checked with the senior operations specialist to see if he had anything to report, then left to make her way to the bridge.

She climbed the steps and entered the dimly lit center of the destroyer to find it quiet, with only murmured conversation breaking the silence. Sarah nodded at the helmsman and the boatswain's mate, neither of whom she recognized, then went to stand by the master chief.

She listened carefully to his report of what had occurred during the previous watch, which included the ship's heading and the present coordinates of the storm and its trajectory. It still appeared to be heading toward them and the data still detailed gale-force winds and heavy seas.

"Are we going to continue on our present heading, Master Chief?" Sarah asked. "Or try to outrun it or change course?"

"That'll be at the captain's discretion, ma'am," the master chief said and glanced at his watch. "He should be here any minute."

At his words, Sarah's stomach lurched and her mouth went dry.

Hell. I'm a bag of nerves even before he's here.

Chapter Thirty-Three

Sarah completed her changeover with the junior officer of the deck, and once she had, she went to the front of the bridge and stood with her back to the room. She didn't want to be close to Jack's chair, but she had no choice. She had to remain where she was.

On time, she heard footsteps sound on the ladder. The master chief said, "Captain on the bridge," and Sarah turned, came to attention briefly then about-faced to look out of the window, her spine stiff and inflexible.

His footsteps drew near and she felt as though she were dying inside. She ignored him when he took his seat beside her. She wasn't going to give him the satisfaction of seeing the hurt on her face. *Let him suffer as much as I am.*

She focused her gaze ahead, although she was barely able to see through the dark. She maintained her position, picked up the binoculars and studied the horizon, sweeping from port to starboard.

The settings of the lenses had been changed to night vision and she was only able to see a green sky, sea and the destroyer's bow. The *BIA* had running lights so other vessels could see her location, but they were not meant to illuminate the deck or other parts of the ship.

Sarah noted that the ocean was still relatively calm, with a sea running at between three and four feet. When she adjusted the lenses and studied the sky, however, there was no moon and a seething mass of clouds boiled overhead.

Sarah had seen the computer weather maps and the satellite images of the approaching storm. The low pressure heading for them was known in nautical terms as a gale. It was predicted to be a thirty-to-forty knot blow, with moderately high waves of approximately eighteen to twenty-five feet.

By comparison to other storms at sea or hurricanes and typhoons, a storm of this strength was nothing more than a blustery rainstorm. Its winds, together with heavy seas, however, could pose a serious problem to a ship, and the destroyer's route and heading had been plotted based on that forecast.

The floor suddenly rolled under her and, off-balance, Sarah grabbed for the arm of Jack's chair to steady herself. Unfortunately, his hand was in the exact same place and her grasp encountered his.

She contorted her body in the opposite direction and released her support, regaining her footing. Her heart jumped into her throat when Jack asked, "You okay?"

Sarah raised the binoculars to her eyes once more and said in a voice that sounded cool and calm, "Absolutely, sir."

She half-turned when the master chief appeared beside Jack. "Heavy weather report, sir," he said. "Our course is zero fifty-two true, speed twenty knots. Gale is seven, sea is four. We have overcast with squalls, and the map indicates the depression is growing in intensity and moving eastward, speed forty knots."

"Very well, Master Chief," Jack replied. "Keep me updated and let's get some precautionary measures in place. I want every hatch dogged and loose gear cleared from the decks. Essential crew only outside. Give the rest something to do below. Everyone is to get their foul-weather gear on."

"Aye, aye, sir," the master chief said. He went to the tannoy system and relayed the message as ordered.

Sarah went to a storage locker and took out her blue foul-weather jacket. She put it on, went back to her position and continued looking out toward the bow. She noted that in the short time since Jack had joined them, the weather had deteriorated markedly.

Waves were now between eight and ten feet in height and they were crashing into the port side. Twenty-knot gusts broke the crests of the boomers into curtains of foam and froth — like so much curdled cream — which floated onto the glass, adhering to and obscuring it. The wind moaned as it snaked along the eaves of the bridge, as if it had developed a life of its own.

The ship suddenly surged forward and rolled to port. Taken by surprise, Sarah staggered, lunged for the shelf but missed and cannoned into Jack's chair.

A supporting hand grasped her arm and, without thinking, she shrugged it off. She steadied herself and glanced sideways at him. He was sitting calmly, as if they were moving through tranquil seas, but his face was pale and his lips were pressed into a thin line.

He was still the Jack she'd fallen in love with, and her heart throbbed with a pain so ferocious that it seemed as if she was being torn apart.

Sarah focused on the horizon again to see that dawn was breaking, although it was not the usual muted citrus overtones of a new day. The distant sky had lightened to a charcoal gray and the clouds churned, stirred to fury by the building strength of the wind.

Her nerves jangled throughout her body. The approaching storm would be her initiation into bad weather while at sea, and she wondered whether she would get seasick or be unable to keep her feet. She could see herself involved in embarrassing and painful faceplanting in front of the watch.

Jack suddenly rose and went to the master chief. "Update, Chief?" he asked.

The chief studied the map screen, which was a kaleidoscope of yellow, burnt orange and spiraling red on a black screen. "Aye, sir. Wind nine, sea five, swells five, bar nine hundred and ninety and falling rapidly, squalls heavy."

"Very well, Chief. I need a report every fifteen minutes. Let's get on top of this bitch."

"Aye, aye, sir."

Sarah glanced over her shoulder and watched as Jack did a circuit of the bridge, speaking to each watch member before he returned to his chair. As he drew close to her, she caught his gaze with her own.

Her cheeks flushed and she managed to drag her eyes from his and faced front. She listened to him move beside her and she brought up the binoculars once more.

The *BIA* suddenly rolled to port, then from midships to her prow, she reared into the air. Sarah staggered backward and grabbed a corner of a computer. Other members of the team swore and she surmised they'd all been caught off guard by the destroyer's sudden maneuver.

She went to the window, walking with her legs apart to keep her balance, and studied the ocean. The waves were now of greater length and had increased in size. They smashed against the hull, threw up fountains of water and shredded sheets of foam and spindrift onto the deck.

The violent movement was followed by an uneven lurch and the ship slewed to starboard. Something pounded her hull and an enormous wave crashed over her bow, the water cascading along the ship to midships.

The ship stabilized for a few seconds before she heeled to port and hurled herself through another huge wave. Sarah lost her footing and fell toward the captain's chair, managing to save herself by grabbing onto the shelf.

The wind had become ferocious and howled like a bestial animal. Pattering like hailstones on plastic broke the silence and the glass was suddenly blurred by heavy rain.

A second later the clear-view screen spun to life and Sarah sighed with relief, because she could continue to do her job by using the piece of armored glass to see through.

It was a hardened glass disk designed for mounting in a hole cut into a ship's window. It spun at one thousand four hundred revolutions per minute, a speed which would continuously throw off rain, snow, ice or spray from the surface of the optically corrected glass to maintain an undistorted outlook.

Sarah saw that the sky had brightened enough for her to see black clouds overhead. Rain beat a heavy tattoo on the glass and the wind screeched around the superstructure as if it wasn't satisfied to pummel the destroyer, but wanted to a find a way in to wreak its vengeance on her crew.

The *BIA* yawed and her bow plunged into the trough of a wave. Sarah tried to maintain her balance and continued looking through the binoculars. She could see nothing but wave after wave crashing into the port side and spilling their contents onto the deck.

The ship rolled first to port then starboard before she lifted herself skyward to climb a huge wave. Her bow to at least the middle of the ship was, once again, out of the water. She plunged downward to bury her prow into the mountainous sea, and Sarah staggered forward then stumbled backward and toppled to the floor.

Chapter Thirty-Four

Sarah had no way of saving herself and she tumbled to the deck. The ship immediately heeled to port, lifted her bow and bucked like a maddened horse, and Sarah discovered that a human body could indeed turn into an out-of-control projectile.

Her bottom skidded on the steel plates and she careened backward and crashed into a steel table behind her. Her left shoulder slammed into one of its legs and the agony was instant.

The pain was white-hot and tore through muscles and nerves. It bit into her neck and traveled up into the back of her skull, and she gritted her teeth to stop herself from screaming out loud.

The destroyer yawed once more, this time to starboard, and Sarah hooked her uninjured arm through the self-same metal leg that had hurt her and hung on, holding her injured limb against her chest.

Jack left his chair and came toward her, the violent movement of the ship causing him to stagger. He crouched beside her and he searched her face.

"Are you okay, Morgan?" he asked. "That was one helluva fall."

Sarah released her grip and, after a first attempt, managed to get herself into a seated position.

"I'm fine, sir," she said, although her shoulder throbbed with a deep and nauseating ache.

"I'll get the doc to come up here and look you over."

Sarah shook her head. "I said I'm fine…sir."

"Sorry, Lieutenant. I'd feel a heck of a lot better if you were checked out."

He half-turned to glance over his shoulder. "Master Chief, get the medical officer up here. Lieutenant Morgan has injured her arm."

"Aye, aye, sir."

While waiting for the ship's surgeon to arrive, Sarah bent her knees and forced the ridged soles of her boots against the shallow grooves in the rectangular steel plates of the floor to keep herself from sliding.

The ship was in constant violent motion. She glanced about her and saw tension on the faces of the watch team. The waves pounding on the destroyer's hull and the repetitive rolling and yawing were taking its toll on them all.

Although the bridge had armored glass and Kevlar plates protecting its interior, the howling wind and torrential rain hammering on the roof were harrowing and set Sarah's teeth on edge.

She only had to wait five minutes for the *BIA*'s doctor to report to the bridge. When he arrived, he crouched beside her and she said loud enough to be heard above the storm lashing the ship, "This is embarrassing. I've only bumped my shoulder."

"We'll see," Lieutenant Winslow replied. "You could've fractured or dislocated it. I'll give it a quick once over. Can you move it okay?"

Sarah followed the doctor's instructions and forced her shoulder and arm into various positions, her teeth clenching with the pain the actions caused. The doctor then examined and manipulated the joint from the injured area to her neck, and while it still hurt her, the sharp, intense agony she'd felt at the initial impact had gone and her range of movement, although restricted, showed there was no major damage.

"I can't seem to find any serious injury, but you've bruised it and it'll hurt like hell for a few days," the doctor said.

He put his hand inside his medical bag and brought out a bottle of water and a strip of pills.

"Here. Take two of these now and a couple in six hours. That should get you over the worst of the trouble."

Sarah took the medication and the container from him, popped the pills from their foil wrapping and swallowed them with a mouthful of liquid.

"Thanks, sir," she said.

Lieutenant Winslow nodded at her and stood. Sarah watched as he lunged his way across the deck until he managed to reach the ladder unscathed.

Jack was at her side as soon as the doctor had left. Without a word, he leaned toward her, gripped her right upper arm and pulled her to her feet.

Sarah recoiled from his grip and said, "I'm okay, sir."

The ship's bow suddenly dipped deep beneath an enormous wave, her stern lifted and Sarah was flung violently forward.

A hand grasped the back of her jacket and Jack brought her up short before she cannoned into the shelf. She gasped, turned to him and saw that he'd anchored himself by holding on to his chair.

Breathless, she nodded her thanks and made her way to her position. She rubbed her shoulder and flexed the joint to ease the pain and hoped the analgesic would kick in quickly.

The clear-view screen was keeping a circular fourteen inches of glass unclouded, but when Sarah tried to see beyond the streaks of rain and foam coating the other windowpanes, she was blind.

The wipers were moving at full speed but visibility was zero. It was the responsibility of radar to warn them if there were other ships in the area, but in the bad weather, anomalies could give false information as to how close other vessels were to them.

Jack spoke behind her and she noted that his voice was clear and strong, with no sign of worry. "Helmsman, get into your safety harness and reduce speed to slow ahead at ten knots."

"Aye, aye, sir."

Despite the rough sea, tiredness and her throbbing arm, Sarah found her ears straining to hear every nuance of his voice, and although the hurt from their split still simmered deep inside her, a wild shiver coursed like hot syrup down her spine and she closed her eyes briefly to regain her composure.

"We've got enough sea room, but we need power to steer through these seas and not get pushed around by wind and waves," Jack continued. "The gale is blowing on the port side, so we have a beam sea. We have to keep her pointing into the waves, since a massive breaker striking the ship's side could roll her over and sink her. The elements will try to turn the vessel, and pushing against them requires forward momentum. Let's do this so we can go home."

Eventually dawn broke, but the arrival of a new morning did nothing to calm her fears. The sight before her was a scene of immense destructive power and her stomach clenched with nerves.

The sky was dark with low, anvil-shaped storm clouds, which boiled like thick smoke. The horizon had vanished behind a charcoal-gray curtain, and heavy rain, mixed with thick foam and spray which streaked the glass panes as if someone had thrown cream paint over them, pounded the windows.

The sea was slate-gray in color, the waves mountainous with crests capped with thick spume and spindrift that showered into the air like discolored snow. They pummeled the port side and over and under the ship's bow, dousing her decks with torrents of water, which crashed against her superstructure.

Each time the *BIA* surged through an enormous breaker, dipped into a trough or scaled a heaving wall of another towering boomer, the ship seemed to shake herself and valiantly plough onward, readying herself for the next pummeling by Mother Nature gone insane.

They were now caught in the teeth of the gale and the wind shook the panes of glass and screamed like something from a horror movie. It battered the ship like a living thing and the destroyer pitched and yawed and swayed in her struggle to survive the onslaught.

Sarah could hear the creak of the warship's steel plates and joints in reaction to the heavy strain and stressors put on them, and she had a horrible vision of the destroyer breaking apart before it sank in a slow spiral to its death on the seabed.

The constant pounding and the heaving of the floor made her grit her teeth, and she leaned forward to hold on to the shelf, her knuckles going white with the force of her grip.

"You look a bit green, Morgan. I hope you're not going to throw up on my bridge."

Jack's voice was low and there was a teasing note in it. Sarah was not amused, because she did, in fact, feel nauseous.

"Wouldn't dream of it, sir," she said.

"Master Chief," Jack said, "is there any recent data on this goddamn weather?"

"Yes, sir. Seas are moderating. Weather conditions are improving, wind speed decreasing. We should see clear skies in an hour or two."

"Outstanding," Jack replied.

Sarah twisted her lips in a grimace. *Thank God.*

She stared through the spinning glass screen and couldn't see much difference in the storm as it hammered the ship. The rain still beat a strident tattoo on the roof and windows and waves crashed and pounded the ship's hull incessantly.

She still found it difficult to keep her feet as the vessel continued to heel hard over to her port side then lift her bow to shake herself at the sky. It looked as if hell had arrived and Sarah wondered how long it would be before the gale turned its fury away from them and went off to wreak havoc elsewhere.

Some thirty minutes later, the master chief brought Jack a further report. "Wind speed is fifteen knots, sir. Conditions are improving with a clearing sky."

Sarah studied a one hundred and eighty-degree arc and saw the horizon, because the weather was indeed clearing. It was still raining heavily, but it was no longer pounding the bridge roof and appeared to be easing off.

The tempest had ceased its demented howl and the breakers had decreased to less than half their previous height.

"Helmsman, increase to half-ahead full, fifteen knots, course zero six six degrees. Let's go home," Jack ordered.

"Aye, aye, sir. Course zero six six, half-ahead full, fifteen knots."

* * * *

Sarah gazed out the windows at a calm and sparkling sea. There was no sign of the gale, which had veered off to expend its fury on pastures new, and small wavelets lapped at the destroyer's hull. There was a clear blue sky and bright sunlight, and her relief at arriving in homeport was enormous.

Sarah half-turned to her left and could see the long wharf of Norfolk Naval Station drawing close as the *BIA* reversed toward her berth. It was good to be home, but she felt a deep sadness, because there was no future for her and Jack and she would be without him.

She was exhausted. The return journey had been uneventful once the storm had retreated. The ship had suffered no damage and neither had the crew, except for a few bruises and a sprained wrist. Her own shoulder throbbed and her body felt battered, but that was all.

Jack had not acknowledged her presence on the bridge in the time it had taken them to sail home. He'd been busy and it was unreasonable of her to think he should have paid any attention to her. Even so, Sarah was confused and her feelings and spirits were low. She'd hoped he would change his mind, but he hadn't summoned her to his quarters and, in her eyes, it was over.

She kept watch through the binoculars to make sure there were no vessels near enough to them to cause a problem. The ship proceeded dead slow astern with two tugboats nudging her to her mooring at pier nine.

Jack issued orders in relation to the docking but she remained disconnected from what was going on around her. The only thing she wanted to do was disembark, get into her car and head for the hotel.

There came a thud from the ship's starboard side as the ship made contact with the pier. The deck vibrated slightly as she moved slow astern to nestle at her mooring.

Sarah heard Jack order, "Finished with engines," before he paused then went on, "Stop engines."

The propellers turned for a short while after the vibration of the deck died to a faint tremor, then complete silence fell on the bridge.

Sarah sighed. In a few minutes, she would head to her room, collect her sea bag, make her escape off the destroyer and get as far away from Jack as she could get. She had a lot of thinking to do and she needed to forget everything that had happened, because her future depended on her making the correct choices about what she wanted to do with her life, based on it now being without him.

Chapter Thirty-Five

The number inscribed on the burnished brass plate fastened at head-height to the oak door read three hundred and sixty. Sarah pressed her fingertips to her forehead, as if by doing so she could rid herself of the chaotic thoughts behind them.

I was going to share this room with him. What am I doing here? Don't I have any pride left?

She thrust a hand deep into the front pocket of her uniform pants and pulled the key card from its depths. She stared at the innocuous blue piece of plastic as if it held a solution to her problem and she nibbled her bottom lip hard enough to make her wince.

The pain distracted her momentarily from the misery lodged in her heart, which had gnawed at her relentlessly, causing her sleepless nights and tormented days.

Did I come here thinking he might show up? He made it clear it was over between us, so why am I still hoping?

Sarah's eyes filled with tears but she blinked them back. She was determined not to give in to the despair that had haunted her since Jack had brought her world crashing around her.

A wave of sadness flooded through her and she bit her lip again. It was a worthless effort because the diversion didn't work. She was humiliated at the way she had given herself to him so easily and without shame, and she hadn't realized how much she loved him.

Heartbreak was no easy fix. She'd opened herself to him only to have her heart crushed, and her soul — which made her who she was — was empty. She believed she had no hope of ever making either of them whole.

He'd taken everything she had of herself and she felt humiliated and used. She was numb and felt like a deer frozen in a vehicle's headlights with no idea how she was going to sort herself out.

It's my own fault. I should have known better. He tried to warn me but I didn't listen.

Sarah struggled valiantly not to whimper like a wounded animal, and lifted her chin. She couldn't dwell on what was unfixable and a surge of determination strengthened her resolve.

Shit! He paid for the room and I have the key card. I might as well put it to good use.

Sarah swiped the plastic through the magnetic machine above the door handle and heard a small click. It swung open a few inches on spring-loaded hinges, and she clutched her sea bag tight and pushed at the barrier to open it wide.

Before she went in, Sarah glanced nervously along the hallway in both directions to see if anybody had appeared on her floor and could see her. Once she'd confirmed there was no one about, she stepped over the threshold.

Inside, she dropped her bag to the floor and gently pushed the door shut with her foot.

The richness and opulence of the room caused her to stare around her in awe and she remained rooted to the spot. The décor was contemporary but elegant, with a thick beige carpet and heavy drapes of the same shade hanging at a large east-facing window and open double doors which led out onto a balcony. The walls, papered in what Sarah thought to be wheaten silk, shimmered in the sunlight flooding through the two large expanses of glass.

A king-sized bed, draped in pristine white linen with pillows piled at the headboard, dominated the space. The air smelled of lemon furniture polish that did battle with various scents from a vase of fresh flowers set in the center of a snow-white monogrammed cloth that draped a round table.

Alongside the blooms were a pair of crystal glasses, beside which was a large gleaming silver bucket containing a bottle of expensive champagne. A silver tray contained neatly aligned bottles of water and the makings for coffee and tea.

My, what an expensive room — and with a bottle of champagne to boot. The Captain is an extravagant man. It puts the room I stayed in on the second floor to shame. I guess I can always do the alcohol justice and get wrecked. It would be a helluva mistake to waste it.

Sarah tried to find humor in her situation — or at least some way of raising her spirits — but she didn't have the heart. Anger stabbed at her tender psyche but was quickly overwhelmed by a deep sense of loss.

She moaned, the sound barely heard in the silence that hung like a heavy shroud in the room. She wanted to rage at Jack and herself so it would wipe out the desolation clawing at her insides, but the fury had disappeared and its absence left her empty.

The bastard thought of everything.

She didn't want to focus on her memories any longer and she picked up her bag and walked toward the bed and set it down. When she noticed how big the piece of furniture was, it sparked another thought.

This thing is certainly large enough for two. It's a joke.

Everything she looked at made her think of Jack. Anguish continued to needle her insides and she went to the balcony doors.

She stepped outside, released her hair from its tightly coiled bun and ran her fingers through the tresses. She shook her head until tousled curls fell onto her shoulders, and went to the railing. She grasped the warm wood and gazed down at the boardwalk before shifting her attention to the beach.

The room was on the seventh floor and Sarah had an uninterrupted view across the vast golden sands to where Jack had rescued her when she'd been attacked.

The sun blazed from a deep blue sky devoid of clouds and bathed everything in a faint apricot glow. Waves rippled on the damp sand and seemed threaded with gold, which sparkled and danced in the sunlight.

As she looked seaward, she noticed the sleek lines of a battleship making its way along the coast on its home run to Naval Station Norfolk. The wake caused by its huge screws churned a frothy, glittering tidal wave for some distance astern. A lone seagull cruised above the ensign, which fluttered in a brisk wind caused by its passage.

Sarah was restless and helpless in equal measure. If she were honest with herself, she didn't want to be there. She wanted *him* to be with her and needed him to make her feel whole once more.

Is he being his usual committed and loyal self, still on the BIA? Or has he gone home?

With a last look at the huge ship, she turned away from the scene, went into the room and stopped. Her thoughts jumped to Jack once more and she wondered again where he was.

She muttered a curse. The emptiness inside her was unbearable and pain twisted like a knife in her chest. It hurt more than she could've ever imagined.

When will I be able to let him go? How can I ever go back to the BIA? I must be so weak. He was never going to be mine and I should've known, but I let him use me.

A small sob escaped her and Sarah covered her face with her hands. She stood immobile for a few moments, her skin hot against her palms, and tried to pull herself together.

At last, she uncovered her face and walked to the bed. She took off her uniform jacket and threw it beside the bag. She unzipped her sea bag and decided to take out her toiletries and have a shower. She might be more relaxed afterward, and could open the bottle of champagne and indulge herself.

She bent over the bag and was rummaging through its depths when she heard a faint noise by the door. She glanced to her left to see what had caused it and suddenly found she couldn't breathe.

Her heart skipped a beat then raced on at breakneck speed. Her body was suddenly boneless, with no strength. Her legs trembled and she thought she might crumple to the floor in a heap.

Chapter Thirty-Six

The door that Sarah had kicked shut must not have closed properly. It was now ajar and Jack stood on the threshold of the room watching her, still in his working uniform. Over the short distance between them, she saw his face was pale, his eyes narrowed and a tiny muscle in his jaw flickered. His hands were fisted at his sides, as if every muscle in his body was stiff with tension.

Sarah's heart pounded so hard that she thought it was going to burst from her chest. At the sight of him, her breath locked in her throat and a surge of love — like a tidal wave — swept through her. The temporary barrier her subconscious had built to protect her from further hurt began to crumble.

What's he doing here?

Jack lifted his chin, and when he spoke his voice was emotionless and cold. "Lieutenant."

Sarah straightened and swallowed. "What are you doing here?" When she spoke, her words were sharp and pierced the silence of the room like splinters of ice.

Jack remained quiet and she continued, "Well, sir, I guess this is your room. I'll get out of your way and leave you to it."

Sarah leaned forward to zip her bag and her hair fell like a curtain about her face. It shielded her from his gaze, which was so intense she imagined it might scorch her skin.

She froze when Jack said, "No. We need to talk."

Sarah couldn't think straight. Questions tore through her mind as to why he was at the hotel and what he wanted to speak to her about. Annoyed at the sheer balls of the man, the hurt she'd been suffering was at last replaced with anger and she welcomed its arrival.

She spun to face him and heat burned her cheeks. She clenched her hands into fists at her sides and she glared at him. "Oh. So *now* you want to talk," she said.

Jack bent and picked something up from the hallway floor. He stepped into the room and kicked the door shut behind him.

Sarah's eyes fell on his brown leather overnight bag and the uniform carrier he held. Confusion replaced her annoyance. However, why he had those items with him was irrelevant and she silently watched him place both on the carpet.

He took two paces toward her. "We've *got* to talk," he repeated.

Sarah shook her head in denial. Ire at his insensitive words that they now needed to talk reinstated itself. "I've nothing to say to you and *you've* already said enough."

She wanted to get away from him as fast as she could. She was tired of being on an emotional rollercoaster where he was concerned. Her head told her to run, but her traitorous heart wanted desperately to hear his reasons for being at the hotel and ordered her to stay. She was rooted to the floor, unable to make her limbs or her feet move so she could escape.

Stubbornness decreed she go and she leaned forward to pick up her jacket. "No. I should go."

Her emotions at war with each other, Sarah watched Jack from out of the corner of her eye for his reaction to her words. He took another pace toward her.

"I was wrong, Sarah. I made a mistake."

Sarah detected a note of pleading in his voice. Her gaze flew to his and she glared at him, wanting to hiss and spit like a very angry cat. "Oh? What mistake did the great Captain Chalmers make that he thinks he needs to apologize to a lowly lieutenant for? An apology for sleeping with me? A 'sorry' for using me? For *fucking* with me?"

Fury boiled inside her as the words spilled from her lips. A voice in her mind begged her to stop before she said something that she might later regret, but it was too late to retract her cruel statement.

Jack brushed his hand through his hair then folded his arms. He stared at her silently, eyes narrowed again, the planes of his face hard.

Sarah saw his anger and knew that if she didn't calm down and choose her words with care, she would throw away any chance she had with him.

She shrugged. "Okay, *Captain*. Say what you came to say then I'll go. I have better things to do."

Oh, let up on him, girl. You're hell bent on destroying any hope you have of leaving with at least a small piece of your heart intact.

Jack was still angry and didn't try to disguise it. "Are you gonna let me speak now? That's mighty nice of you."

Sarah couldn't meet his eyes and stared intently at the toe of her boot. "Don't put this all on me, Jack. I'm the fool who convinced herself that we had something good. *You* screwed it up."

Jack sighed but remained silent, and she wondered if he'd decided not to bother with her.

At last he spoke, although his words sounded hesitant. "That night in my quarters...when I told you it was over? I made the biggest mistake of my life. As soon as I'd said those words to you, I knew I'd screwed up. I realized I couldn't live without you and, even more crap, that *my* job would be fucked anyway because I'd be a head case. When you left, I wanted to call you back and make things right, but it was too late.

"I'm still committed to the Navy. That won't ever change. And I still maintain it will be my fault if your career gets screwed and you lose any chance you might have to be the best at what you do." His lips twisted in a grimace. "Holy shit. I'm talking such a load of bull."

Sarah was stunned. She wondered whether she'd opened the champagne in her sleep and had drunk the whole bottle.

Maybe I'm lying on the bed wasted and everything I'm hearing is a figment of my imagination.

She still wasn't prepared to back down and wouldn't look at him.

Jack continued, "When I said what I did and you left, I knew I'd lost you and it almost drove me crazy."

Hearing the raw emotion in his voice, Sarah looked at him and saw he'd moved to within a few feet of her.

His usual deadpan expression had vanished, replaced with one of unhappiness and longing.

A tear trickled down her face and her voice shook as she said, "You hurt me so much, Jack."

"Oh, Christ, Sarah. Please don't cry."

"Jack—" He was only a few paces away from her and the words she was trying to say faded from her mind. He was too close for comfort and the bed was in the way, which stopped her retreat.

She held her hand up, palm outward, to stop him from moving any closer.

"Don't send me away," Jack said quietly. "You've got to give me another chance, Sarah."

Sarah loved and wanted him. There was no artifice or denial in the thought. She craved him, but his cruel rejection of her was like a black chancre where her heart was. It needed to be cauterized before she could move on.

Her anger fled and she said softly, "I can't, Jack. You made it clear things could never work out between us, that there'd be too many complications for you if we had a relationship. I get the rules about fraternization and the fact you're my commanding officer—and a senior-ranking one at that. If the brass found out about us, the consequences would be dire and neither of us would come back from them. You knew that, but you...*we* still went ahead with something that was wrong. You dumped me because you considered your career was more important than us. You were right. It wouldn't work."

Jack's voice rose as he spoke. "I know what I said. I hurt you and it made me feel like the biggest shit ever."

Sarah knew she should let things go, but she couldn't. "So now you have a guilty conscience and want to make amends?"

Jack shook his head, a bleak expression on his face. "No. C'mon, Sarah. Gimme a break. I want you. I want *us*. That's why I'm here. Fuck my high-assed ideas of what's right or wrong. Yeah, I know what the outcome will be, but I'm willing to go with it rather than lose you. Listen... I said I'm sorry. I made a mistake. I hurt you but I'm not going to grovel and beg for your forgiveness. If you don't believe me then I'm gone."

Sarah heard the irritation in his voice and was positive he'd never been in a situation like this before, where he'd made a wrong choice and needed to rectify it. He'd set such high standards for himself during his life and had kept himself apart from affairs of the heart because of it.

No matter how much he'd hurt her, she couldn't continue to blame him. Being dedicated to his job wasn't a crime. She'd known the consequences of getting involved with him. Laying the blame at his feet because he'd been stronger than her went against what she believed was right and wrong. She also knew she was backing him into a corner as some form of revenge and if she continued to do so, he would leave.

He wasn't the type of man to be emotionally blackmailed or humbled because of a mistake. What was done was done. There was no point in dwelling on the past. She could forgive and move on with him or turn him away.

He had his reasons and I need to forgive him, otherwise I'll have nothing. To hell with rules and regulations. The Navy can rot, because I love him. If I let him go, I'll regret it for the rest of my life.

Sarah took a single pace toward him. The next ones were easier because she went willingly. The hurt was still there, twisting in her belly, but it was at a level she could deal with now he was with her.

Jack met her and when they came together, his arms went around her in the intimate and demanding way she'd come to love and need. He held her tight, as if he never wanted to let her go again, and her body thrilled at his touch. She clasped her hands behind his head and pressed herself against him.

Chapter Thirty-Seven

Jack and Sarah stared at each other, their mouths so close that she could feel his warm breath on her lips. She wanted him to kiss her so his need for her could wipe out the hurt that had consumed her over the last few days. She thought it was only then that she would start to heal.

The corner of Jack's mouth lifted in the way that set her pulse racing, and as though he could read her mind, he touched her lips with his.

He teased their softness before he drew back and said, "I love you, Sarah. I'm never going to let you go again. There's nothing in this world that means more to me than you. I'm no good with fancy romantic words, so this is going to sound like so much bull crap. I've loved you from the moment I saw you. I should've told you a long time ago. I almost did by the lake at my parents' place but Hayley interrupted us. I can't change what I've done to you. There are no words that I can say that'll do that. If I were in your shoes, *I* wouldn't forgive me. Give me a chance to make it up to you and I will."

Jack cupped her chin in his hand and his gaze held hers, as though waiting for a response.

Sarah's mind spun. She'd heard the words clearly enough, but they'd sounded like they'd been spoken in a dream and she couldn't process what he'd said.

She settled her gaze on his eyes. The old saying was that they were the windows to the soul. In this case, they were, and when she saw the truth in them, her own filled with tears and a small sob escaped her.

He does *love me.*

Jack's expression changed to one of bemusement. "Why're you crying?" he asked. "Shit. I thought I'd make you happy."

Sarah wiped away a rogue tear with a trembling hand. Her voice was tremulous when she said, "I *am* happy. I love *you*, Jack. I can't remember when I didn't. I'm just... I don't know what to think because I can't believe you feel the same. You've never said a word. I hoped you did, but with everything you've said...and done—"

Jack stopped her with a slow and tender kiss. When he drew back, he smiled. "I guess you are happy, then."

As her answer, Sarah kissed him on his mouth, his nose and finally his jaw. Jack's mouth met hers in a searing kiss and delight coursed through her.

As with their previous kisses, their passion flared—quick and hot—but Jack pulled back from her lips. "No way," he murmured and he tightened his arms about her.

Sarah nibbled at his bottom lip before she said, "You love it."

"Yeah," he replied and proceeded to show her how much he did, kissing her forcefully before he licked her bottom lip. He skimmed his hands along her spine to caress her bottom, then he glided his palms around to her stomach.

Sarah gasped at his touch. A fire ignited in her lower belly and she moaned.

Jack stopped his breathing ragged. "Whoa," he said, "we need to stop."

Sarah sighed and rested her head on his shoulder. She inhaled the scent of him and pushed her hips against his erection. "I can feel you," she said.

Jack moved against her in turn. "Uh-huh. That can wait. I need to tell you something."

Sarah wanted him to kiss her again but raised her head so she could stare into his face. "What's that?"

Jack hesitated as though nervous, then said, "I'm going to resign my commission."

Sarah was so cocooned in the warm feeling that being back in his arms had triggered that at first his words didn't register with her. Then their meaning hit her hard. His statement was so surprising and unexpected that she needed it clarified.

She leaned back in the circle of his arms and studied him intently. "What did you say?"

His eyes had darkened to a turbulent blue, a sign that his decision had not been an easy one. In fact, knowing him as well as she did, she knew the struggle he would undoubtedly have had. Even though there was resolve in his voice, the emotion in his gaze told her he was unhappy with his choice and her stomach sank.

Jack must have noticed her shock, but before she could speak, he continued, "Hear me out, okay? The shakedown patrol we've just come back from? It was hell. When you fell on the bridge during the storm and hurt yourself, I wanted to be like a normal guy helping his girl but I couldn't do a damn thing. I *hated* you being on the ship in the bad weather. I knew the *BIA* could get through it with no problems and so could the crew and even you. But if anything had gone wrong and something *had* happened to you, I wouldn't have been able to live with myself."

Jack ran a hand through his hair and, for the first time, Sarah saw him show signs of agitation. "Look… Onboard ship, we'll have to spend twenty-four hours a day together. How the hell will we be able to act like we don't mean anything to each other? It's only going to be a matter of time before a member of the crew gets suspicious. Chad Mason has figured it out and he's already hauled me over the coals about it. I listened to him and I shouldn't have. I was an asshole.

"I'm a grown man, but it *really* eats at me when I see the guys flirt with you. I love you and it hit me when I realized that I don't give a flying fuck about my career. I'd much rather resign and be with you than lose you."

When Sarah heard the vehemence in his voice, she caressed his clenched jaw before she glided her hands behind his head once more.

She shook her head. "You make a good argument, Jack," she said, "but you can't resign. While it's your decision, I won't let you. I'd feel as guilty as hell if you gave up everything for me. It wouldn't do either of us any good. The Navy needs you, Jack. You've achieved so much. What you've done has gotten you where you are now. You can't throw it all away for me. Besides, you can't just walk away overnight. They'll have to release you from your contract and that'll take at least a year — if they let you go at all. Veteran captains are as rare as flying pigs. Even more so when they've got your experience.

Jack grimaced then looked annoyed. "Well, give me a solution then, because I don't have one."

Sarah moved her hands from the back of his head and along his shoulders to his chest. She flattened her palms and rubbed the material of his jacket.

I would do anything for him.

She took a deep breath then let it out. Her mind drifted. She couldn't let him walk away from something that meant so much to him and that he was so good at.

If she put aside the problems their relationship would face if they stayed together, she knew he would be unhappy with civilian life. He loved her now, but what would happen if he grew to hate her because she'd come between his commitment and loyalty to his job?

There was an alternative, but it meant sacrificing her own career. Was being with him and setting aside her own dreams and goals more important? Would *she* be able to come to terms with her decision and walk away from a lifestyle that she loved? But the real question was did she love that lifestyle more than she loved him?

Her heart felt like it was tearing in two with the import of having to make one hell of a choice. She knew that she loved him. There was no doubt there. The thought of being without him — of letting him go or accepting his own decision to resign — was untenable. Then she focused on the fact that he was fully prepared to give it all up for her — to be with her.

There was only one way out. She came to a decision that she knew was impulsive and one she'd thought she would never have to make. Not giving herself a chance to change her mind, she said, "*I'll* resign from the Navy."

As she heard herself utter the shocking words, a sharp pang of sadness together with an acute sense of failure knotted her stomach. She was quick to dismiss the feelings. She knew she wouldn't have been human if she hadn't experienced some form of emotion at having to make such an important decision without proper thought.

She accepted it, however, because it was the right thing to do. A sacrifice to save their love so they could be together needed to be made and she could do it far more easily then Jack. She warmed at the reminder that he was willing to make that sacrifice for her, and his would be much more difficult and meaningful than what she would be giving up.

Jack's body stiffened against hers. "Shit. No way, Sarah," he said. "The same applies. How do you think *I'm* going to feel if you go ahead with that? You've got your whole career ahead of you. You can't just give it up."

Sarah rested her hands on his stomach and rubbed the firm muscles to calm him down. "It's not a done deal then. After all this, we can't even reach a compromise or work it out. So, what do we do?"

She knew she'd distracted him with her touch because he hissed through gritted teeth before he blew out a gust of air.

Sarah forced herself to smile and continued to massage his stomach. "As soon as my own tour is up, I could get a job landside on the station. They're crying out for ex-serving civilians to take up posts as security specialists. I had a desk job before I applied for a transfer to sea duty, so I'm qualified."

Excitement stirred in Sarah's stomach. The more she focused on the fact that she might still have a challenging future and she would have Jack as well, the more at peace she felt with her decision. *It could be the best of all worlds.*

"Some of the jobs are not exactly stimulating, but I could go for more qualifications. That way we could be together whenever you're in homeport. That's so much better than not being with each other at all."

Jack stayed quiet. She studied his face and wished she knew what he was thinking.

"I love you, Jack," she continued softly and persuasively. "I nearly lost you once. If it happens a second time, there wouldn't be anything left anyway. Trust me. I wouldn't have said what I did if I had any doubts or if I didn't believe it's the right thing to do. Anyway, don't be so full of yourself. I'll still have a career, just not the one I started out in."

Jack gazed over the top of her head, his expression one of stubbornness. Sarah waited for his answer and at last, he stared into her face and shook his head. "I don't like it, Sarah. In fact, I hate that we're even thinking along those lines."

"Look at it this way then," Sarah continued. "What if we have children?" She blushed at the thought. "I'd have to take leave of some kind — or would you want our kids palmed off onto strangers while we went back to sea? That would also give us problems, as it would be unpaid and only amounts to six weeks after childbirth."

Jack was silent again then said in a harsh voice "It's not about money. We'd be able to manage if you didn't work."

Sarah sighed. "I know that, Jack. I'm not talking about money. I'm using it as an example for justifying why it's common sense for me to be the one to resign. Anyway, if we're going down the route of talking about bucks, your paycheck is a lot bigger than mine."

Jack stared at her, his expression resolute, as though he still disagreed with what she'd said. "I don't want you to be unhappy with your decision."

"We'd have each other," Sarah said. "Yeah, it'll be hard for me. I'll be honest. But I'll suck it up and get over it because we'll be together. After all, you were willing to resign for me."

Jack's body relaxed and his expression became warm. "You're so goddamn stubborn—and very persuasive," he said.

Sarah smiled. "I've already told you. It's part of my resume, so you'll have to deal with it."

"Why don't we leave it for now and we can talk some more?" Jack said. He still sounded unconvinced.

Sarah shook her head. "No. You'll try to change my mind. I've made my decision and I'm not going back on it."

Jack growled, a sign of impatience. "Shit. Okay. I can be a stubborn son-of-a-bitch as well. If you're gonna resign, we'll get married."

Sarah's heart stopped for a single beat then raced on. Happiness at his words coursed through her body and she fought back the tears. "You're going over the top a bit, Jack. Don't ask me to marry you for that reason alone."

Jack shook her. "I'd marry you because I love you, Sarah," he said. "I want you to be my wife. That way there'll be no more bullshit pretending that we aren't involved. We won't have to keep away from each other or worry about getting reamed out by the Navy. I want to know you'll be there when I come home. I know that being apart will suck, especially for you, but we'll be together."

Sarah laughed. "Why, Jack Chalmers... Are you seriously proposing to me?"

"Yeah, I guess I am. It's not romantic and I'm sure it must be one of the shittiest proposals ever made, but will you...? Marry me, I mean?"

There was a boyish expression on his face and she felt a rush of exhilaration. "Yes," she said tremulously. "Yes. Yes. Yes."

She tightened her arms around his neck and Jack picked her up and held her close. His mouth met hers and the searing urgency of his lips conveyed the truth of his words and of the question he'd asked her.

As the desire swelled in her, a flaring beacon of hope for their future flooded through her. He was hers.

She would be Jack's wife. That would bring her a far more important and fulfilling role than her naval one. It was the one that mattered the most. Whatever their future held, love would bind them together and to see them through.

Jack nuzzled her face, successfully distracting her and sending her thoughts whipping away to the back of her mind. "So," he murmured, "are we gonna put this bed to good use?"

Sarah met his lips in a chaste kiss. "Of course. It would be such a goddamn shame to waste it... Captain."

Want to see more from this author? Here's a taster for you to enjoy!

Willing to Surrender
Sharon Kimbra Walsh

Excerpt

1993

Annie McKendrick had begun her graduation day by joining four hundred and ninety-seven other seniors from Langley High School in McLean, Virginia, in boarding the yellow school buses provided to take them to Constitution Hall, which was located on the outskirts of the expansive grounds.

She could still picture the glowing faces of the students on her coach and the singing and chanting that had erupted from everyone — including herself — during the ten-minute journey. The excitement had continued, even once they'd arrived outside the imposing, pale-gray stone building with its numerous columns supporting a decorative mansard roof where cheering families and friends had met them.

Just being inside the ornate building's time-honored halls, with its pristine white walls and arched, green carved-and-decorated ceilings and paintwork, had made Annie feel as if she were in a dream. At one point, she had wondered when the bubble would burst and she would wake up.

The two-hour ceremony had passed in a kaleidoscope of noise and color. She'd mounted the stage to receive her diploma, posed for official photographs and had thereafter searched for and found her parents to have more pictures taken with them and her friends.

The emotions she'd felt had been beyond what she'd expected, but the argument she'd had afterward with her boyfriend, Cory Anderson, had briefly dampened her mood and, for a time, had soured her enthusiasm for the upcoming evening festivities.

The quarrel had been about her parents, who were going on vacation the next day. Annie wouldn't be seeing them for a considerable period of time, so she'd decided that she would spend the intervening hours between the ceremony that morning and the celebrations in the evening with them.

Cory hadn't been amused when she'd told him she wouldn't be traveling with him and their friends to the elegant high-rise Ritz-Carlton Hotel at Tyson's Corner where the graduation celebration was to take place.

His familiar tactic of using emotional blackmail to get her to do what he wanted hadn't succeeded, and when she'd refused to back down, he'd exploded. The disagreement that had ensued as a result had tested her patience and resolve, and, at that point, she'd almost ended their relationship.

Annie sighed and eyed the littered tabletop. Thirsty, she searched for her glass of iced water and, after a few moments, found it among the other half-consumed and empty ones crowded together on the surface. She took a sip of the cold liquid and sighed when chilled moisture doused her throat and eased its dryness.

She set the glass back on the table and glanced around to see if she could find Cory. He was nowhere to be seen, and his absence made her feel more irritated than hurt that he'd left her alone to entertain herself.

She'd been dating him for six months. He was a typical all-American boy and had been captain of the high school soccer team. He was good-looking and more than aware of it, but of more concern to Annie's peace of mind was that he was a flirt and didn't give a damn that she knew it.

A short time into their relationship, she had noticed that his charming and appealing manner — very evident when he was in front of his peers or people he thought he needed to impress — was nothing but a veneer to cover his true personality.

He could be arrogant and self-centered, and she'd learned the hard way that he was used to getting his own way. He threw spectacular tantrums when he didn't get the attention he believed he deserved, which always left her feeling drained and numb, as though she'd spent time with an out-of-control, recalcitrant child who had no idea how to behave.

They were character traits that didn't sit well with her. In fact, they showed a side of him she didn't like at all. She'd begun to wonder what she saw in him.

Despite her growing unease, she hadn't wanted to give up on their relationship, but in recent weeks, she had grown irritated and frustrated with the way things were going between them. When she'd found herself making excuses for his behavior to other people, she'd stopped indulging his outbursts.

Thinking about him was making Annie feel uncomfortable, so she let her thoughts drift and studied her surroundings.

The graduation celebration was in full swing. The dance floor was crowded with energetic men and women who seemed to be out to impress each other with their antics. Some of the gyrations were extraordinary, and she smiled to herself and wondered if their acrobatic and somewhat ludicrous moves would be remembered with embarrassment the next day.

The room was a classic formal ballroom with a décor in antique gold and cream and wall-to-wall carpet of the same colors. It was opulent and elegant without being vulgar. Crystal chandeliers hung from an oval-domed ceiling that was carved with Victorian tracery, and lit sconces lined the walls, which were papered in silk and accented with crown molding.

Panoramic windows were festooned with sheer cream drapes, and there were soft brocade seats set around gilt-edged tables and antique credenzas positioned at strategic points about the room with tall, carved cream vases in their centers, holding cascades of gold-and-ivory flowers.

It was a luxurious and beautiful venue, but Annie was restless. She glanced at her watch and saw it was almost midnight. The noise from the music, raucous conversation and outbursts of laughter were almost deafening, and while she'd spent most of the night dancing, she now had the beginnings of a headache and her feet hurt.

Much against her will, she wondered again where Cory had disappeared to. He'd been acting out of character all evening, and while she suspected he might still be sulking from their earlier argument, her intuition told her it was a little more serious than him acting like a spoiled child.

After all, they hadn't parted on the best of terms, and even now, Annie was still annoyed with him. On this day of all days, his fit of angst had made her resent his behavior, and she'd had a sinking feeling that things between them weren't going as well as they should.

Annie wondered what would happen between them when she left for her basic training. She'd joined the Medical Corp of the United States Army, and in a few weeks' time, she would travel from her home nine hundred and forty-four miles to Fort Leonard Wood in Missouri, where she would begin her sixteen-week gender-integrated basic combat training.

If she passed that, she would move on to Fort Sam Houston to commence her medical and advanced courses to become a specialist in her trade. That could last anywhere from sixteen to sixty-eight weeks, depending on any additional skills she wanted to learn.

Annie hadn't chosen her career lightly or taken the step to sign up without a good degree of soul-searching. She'd understood that what lay ahead of her might well be filled with pitfalls and setbacks.

She would soon be leaving her family, Cory and her hometown, where she had lived all her life. While her parents supported her career choice wholeheartedly, Cory had neither given her his support nor shown any interest.

He hadn't told her he would miss her, and she had a feeling that once she was gone, he would move on to someone new. If she were honest with herself, she'd admit it dented her pride rather than her heart to think that once she was out of his sight, she would also be gone from his mind.

Why the hell am I thinking about that time-waster?

Annie pushed thoughts of her boyfriend to the back of her mind. She was eighteen years old and the world was her oyster. She was free of school at last and her future stretched ahead of her, an infinite highway of hope and adventure. She was going to grab onto it with both hands and look back only when she needed to.

Then thoughts of him intruded into her mind and a trickle of warmth trailed down her spine when she thought of the incident which had occurred outside the hotel after her father had dropped her off to wait on the forecourt for Cory and their friends to arrive.

She'd noticed a gleaming black limousine with tinted windows pull up in front of her and her curiosity had been aroused, even though it had been no more impressive than the other automobiles dropping off their passengers. She wasn't normally a nosey person, but she'd stared at the windows to see if she could see inside and recognize its occupants.

The rear, left-hand passenger door had opened and a man in formal evening dress had gotten out. The sound of female laughter had come from its interior, and she'd watched as he leaned forward and reached out a hand to whomever was inside.

Her interest had been piqued even more when he'd assisted a young woman of about her own age to alight. A second man, followed by another woman, had appeared from the opposite side and she'd wondered who they were.

The man who had exited first appeared older than the rest of his group and she'd continued to stare as they slammed the doors shut and the two couples moved toward the sidewalk.

Annie had realized her interest was bordering on rudeness, and she'd been about to focus her attention elsewhere when the stranger had turned and had caught her studying them. Like an animal trapped in the glare of a car's headlights, she'd stiffened and a wave of embarrassment had surged through her.

Her face had flushed with heat, but instead of ignoring the man like she should have done, she'd chosen instead to return his look. She'd felt a jolt of recognition.

Home of Erotic Romance

Sign up for our newsletter and find out about all our romance book releases, eBook sales and promotions, sneak peeks and FREE romance books!

About the Author

Sharon spent eight and a half years in the Women's Royal Air Force. Originally based in London, after she met her husband, Sharon relocated to Scotland to settle in Edinburgh. Already loving the country after having been stationed there during her time in the military, Sharon has never looked back. She lives with her husband and rescue West Highland Terrier, Snowie, (who thinks that she is a Rottweiler in disguise).

In 2014 Sharon started to have visions of writing a contemporary military romance. The ideas started to pile up and there was nothing for it but to get them down on her laptop, regardless of time and place.

Sharon loves to hear from readers. You can find her contact information, website details and author profile page at https://www.totallybound.com